WORLD BUILDER

Short Fiction Anthology

Evan Gillespie

To my wife Chelsey and our girls Rylee, Isabel, Sadie, and Ella.
Thank you for building this amazing world with me.

I'd also like to thank iPads and Chelsey's naps. You kept
everyone distracted long enough for me to write this book.

CONTENTS

INTRODUCTION

I want to say it had been my dream to create World Builder from an early age, but that's simply not true. If I'm being honest, it came from a place of frustration when I felt like an outsider who may never find his way into the writing world. From 2000 - 2008 I worked in the food service/restaurant industry, which, if you don't know, sucks. I've been a waiter, a line cook, and later worked my way up to a manager. I even have an unfinished hotel/restaurant management degree to go along with it. In my early days of cooking in the kitchen, I remember keeping an ongoing manuscript hidden in the bread cabinet that I would work on between orders. The manuscript wasn't for World Builder but a science fiction film script titled Atonement. I lived, breathed, and dreamed the story for months. I was obsessed.

When I finally finished placing the last period on the script, I thought, "I've done it!" Surely some major film studio will knock on my front door and beg to pay me millions of dollars, and I will never have to make another house salad again! Tragically, that did not happen. I sent numerous queries to agents, only to get mostly crickets and a few auto-generated "no thank you's." I eventually pivoted and decided to turn the script into a novel. I decided to write a book that would clearly be picked up and published, and then the major studios would come calling, asking/pleading for me to let them turn the book into a major motion picture, which I had already written! Tragically, yet again, that did not happen. I also clearly remember being in the movie theater, seeing a trailer for the war film Atonement, and yelling at the screen that someone had stolen my title. I later learned that the book the film was based on was written a few years before I finished my script. What does all this have to do with a short fiction anthology? Hang in there. I have a moral to this story I'm cooking up.

In 2006, I met my wife while working at a family steakhouse called Sagebrush in Fletcher, NC. It's since closed down, but you can still see the building as of June 2023. I joined the US Air Force in 2009, and writing got put on the back burner with a few low-impact projects over the next ten years while my wife and I grew our family. In 2020, during the Covid pandemic, our family moved to Florida, and life got a bit rough for me. I won't ask you to grab a box of tissues, and please don't feel sorry for me (many people were having a rough time), but I was dealing with a lot of anxiety and feeling isolated and alone. I was fortunate to work with Gary Westfal, a "most interesting man in the world" type, who happens to be a published author. He was a tremendous mentor to me and helped reignite my passion for writing. At the same time, writing became an outlet that got me through some dark times. I became re-obsessed with my Atonement novel, rewrote it, took it from 80k to 155k words, and renamed it The Endless Night. I was on a roll. Surely, after finishing the remastered edition in 2021, I could get an agent to pick up the book, and I would finally make my millions, right? Right??? Once again, the agents decided not to call.

I didn't want to give up, slow down, or put my writing ambitions on hold any longer, so I started looking for short fiction writing competitions that I could jump into without months-long commitment. I also figured getting a few accolades would make me more marketable to a potential agent. After a year of different writing contests and other stories I had written over the years, I had amassed a sizable collection of fiction. And thus, is the birth of World Builder. I've decided to self-publish my collection of short fiction and go from there. I've got many stories to tell, and more publishing options are available to aspiring authors than ever before. The path to this moment has been fascinating, with more plot twists and surprises than any story I could imagine, but I find myself grateful. I've matured, gained a little wisdom, and discovered new perspectives over the years that have all fed back into my writing. And now the moral: whether creating art, forming relationships, or working on ourselves, we should never give up but always keep building.

This anthology contains twenty-one stories of a wild variety, like a sampling of the thoughts and images constantly bouncing around inside my brain. You're going to meet many of my creations, including immortal beings, androids, serial killers, warring apple farmers, and the demons we face, both inside and out. Some stories will be self-contained, while others are the first in a series. Several might be a taste of future novels to come. I've divided the book into five genres: science fiction, fantasy, horror (the trinity of my writing interests), historical drama, and satire. Hopefully, these categories will give the illusion I'm an organized person and also help you get into the right headspace before you start a story. And with that, let's begin.

I. FANTASY

"Fantasy is hardly an escape from reality. It's a way of understanding it." -Lloyd Alexander

THE SEVEN WORDS
THAT KILLED A GOD

S ilveus plucked the world from the cosmos and crushed it in his hand. Six billion sentient lives were snuffed out in an instant. Animals and plants, beyond counting, went along with them. Silveus held his clenched fist over his workbench and worked his fingers in his palm, sprinkling stardust onto the flat wooden table, rubbed smooth by eons of use.

"Ungrateful," he scolded the pile of remains, dipping his other hand into the bowl of Lifewater.

Silveus sprinkled the shimmering liquid into the dust, working and needing the mixture back into a moldable clay.

"Again, Silveus?" a rich voice said from behind his left shoulder.

Silveus turned to see Narathema shaking his head in disapproval. Narathema had golden hair that flowed behind him like a river, strong bronze muscles, and shooting stars trapped within emerald eyes.

"It's easy for you to say, Narathema," Silveus replied. "You are loved on all your worlds."

"Not all," he smiled warmly. "Sometimes my children choose a different path. I will admit, in the end, most find their way back to me."

"Like I said," Silveus grumbled. "These fools," he motioned to the fresh clay, "they had forgotten me entirely. They were fighting over two imaginary gods named Volgrin and Awney! They were killing each other over their own creations!"

"And now they are returned to the clay, never to pray again," Narathema said solemnly.

"It's my right to start over!" Silveus snapped. "I am a God of Creation, just like you."

"This is true," Narathema acknowledged. "But perhaps mercy is the key ingredient you have been missing."

"I'll keep trying until I get it right," Silveus snapped. *Who was Narathema to tell him how to rule his worlds?* "We can't all be as lucky as you."

Silveus looked up from his desk and studied the spherical cosmos as it expanded and contracted before him. The universe filled the Chamber of the Gods, surrounded by ten desks for the ten creators. Falanthia sat to his left, speaking softly to the followers of a newly created world, giving her children the first steps in a multi-million-years journey. Silveus had so few worlds now. There had been so many disappointments. He realized Narathema was still standing close by.

"What do you want?" Silveus asked curtly as he formed the clay back into a sphere.

"How would you like to make a wager?" Narathema asked, drawing the attention of the other gods.

A bet between gods did not happen often. The last time it did, Glathmariel and Bendeesu set two worlds on a collision course to see if their respective civilization could evolve fast enough to avert their destruction. Neither world had survived.

"Speak your terms," Silveus said nonchalantly.

"We will each make a planet inhabited with the same flora and fauna, and let's say one million sentient beings," Narathema began. "We will let them know we are their creator. Then, we must let the other god speak seven words to see if they may win your followers over to their side. We must not touch either world again until ten billion years have passed. The winner may take one of the loser's worlds as their own. "

Silveus pondered the wager for several thousand years. Narathema had so many successful worlds to lose, and Silveus had so little. He could find no compelling reason to reject the offer.

"What if there is no clear winner?" asked Silveus.

"Then we shall wait for another ten billion," Narathema replied.

"I accept," Silveus said at last.

The two worlds were made as agreed, and Silveus finished creating his sentient beings. He spoke to their minds, making his presence known, letting them know he was their creator, and he alone should be worshipped until the end of time. When he was done, he left the tiny globe floating in the empty blackness of space on one side of the cosmos, while Narathema did the same on the other side of the room. They crossed paths as they made their way to speak their seven words. By the time Silveus got to Narathema's planet, he had decided what to say.

Silveus leaned into the tiny marble of new life, projected his thoughts into the minds of every sentient being, and spoke. "Kill all who worship Narathema. Follow Silveus." He smiled as he rejoined Narathema at the entrance to the Chamber of the Gods.

"So, what did *you* say?" Silveus asked wryly.

Narathema only smiled, sitting down on the floor. He motioned for Silveus to join him. The two gods kneeled before the cosmos with their backs to a set of heavy oak doors trimmed in gold. The other eight gods turned their eyes from their own worlds and focused on Narathema and Silveus to watch them finish their pact.

"Before the eyes of the ten, I will let the new world continue without interference for ten billion years," Narathema said. "On my life, I swear it." He turned to look at Silveus.

Never to be outdone, Silveus held his head up high. "Before the eyes of the ten, I will let the new world continue without interference for ten billion years," his voice boomed. "On my life, I swear it."

The other gods nodded their witnessing and turned back to their own worlds, pushing and pulling their creations as their machinations played out across time. Narathema and Savlus sat in silence, watching the cosmos. They waited as the centuries passed like grains of sand through an hourglass.

Both worlds grew and evolved over millions of years, though Narathema's world developed two distinct warring religious factions that worshipped either Silveus or Narathema. The battles raged for generations as both sides pushed the boundaries of technology only to better fight and kill the other. To Silveus's horror, Narathema's followers eventually gained the upper hand in the war, unseating the followers of Silveus and restoring the planet to a state of equilibrium. Those that remained loyal to Silveus, though a small group, maintained their loyalty, and their numbers slowly grew. He had not yet lost to Narathema.

Back on Silveus's world, his people embraced scientific advancement, pushing the boundaries of what the brightest minds even thought was possible. Whatever Narathema had told them had put a hunger in them towards something great, but Silveus was not sure exactly what. Narathema and Silveus stayed seated together on the floor and waited another billion years. Silveus observed, with a growing fascination, that complex modes of thinking had consolidated and focused on inter-dimensional travel. For thousands of years, his planet researched ways to bend the planes of space and time, tapping into the same energies that governed all life in the cosmos, even for the gods. While Silveus would never admit it, it was interesting to see the result of two gods removing their guiding influence from the cosmos. Many worlds thrived, with exploratory vessels traveling and mapping the universe, discovering ancient planets, and starting new connections with other civilizations.

Eventually, a prophecy began and continued over the course of five thousand years, promising the birth of a man that would learn to pierce the veil between worlds. It was almost two billion years after the planet's initial creation that Aetheon Harrsole was born. Taking up the research of his father's legacy, he committed his life to reaching beyond the known world. Aetheon was thirty-two years old when he created the Void

Spear and used it to cut a tear into the dimensional fabric of existence. As Aetheon slipped beyond Silveus's sight, a terrifying chill crept inside the god's heart. Where had the mortal gone?

There was a slow creaking of hinges as the heavy wooden doors to the Chamber of the Gods opened for the first time in a trillion years. Silveus knew that somehow, Aetheon had made his way to their chambers. Narathema and Silveus turned to look back as Aetheon stood tall, holding the Void Spear in one hand.

"Which one of you is Narathema?" Aetheon demanded.

Narathema stood and faced the man. "I am Narathema," he said.

Aetheon nodded, raised the spear, then threw it as a mighty roar escaped his lips. His cry echoed around the chamber as the spear tore through Silveus's chest, bursting out from his side as the force of the impact pushed him backward onto the cold stone floor.

Silveus pawed futilely at the floor, trying to drag himself to his desk, yet he already knew a killing blow had been struck. To feel a sense of mortality for the first time terrified him, a feeling he had never imagined was possible. Warm viscous liquid spilled from his wound, soaking his robes and pooling onto the stone.

"How...," Silveus whimpered.

Did you know that I was the first of us?" Narathema asked. "I awoke in this chamber, alone, staring into black emptiness. Back then, it was nothing more than a small tomb." He waved one hand at the cosmos. "With chisel and hammer, I shaped and expanded this place.

"Tell me what you said," Silveus pleaded, looking to Narathema. "What did you say to my world?"

Narathema ignored him for a moment, a look of ancient nostalgia in his eyes. "You were once one of my children, Silveus. All of you were," he said, nodding at the other gods, the eight of them watching in surprised horror as they peeked around from the edges of the cosmos. "Time and chance brought each of you to me, eventually."

"Please," Silveus winced. "Please. The words."

Narathema kneeled beside Silveus on the ground. "You will become a God of Creation."

"That...that's it?" Silveus laughed bitterly, feeling his essence draining from the wound in his chest.

"That's it," Narathema said. "But it's also everything."

"I don't...I don't...understand," Silveus said, his voice wavering.

"Once your people knew it could be done, it was only a matter of time before they found a way," Narathema said. "It only took a couple billion years."

Silveus rolled onto his back, his chest rising and falling quickly.

Narathema looked on Silveus with pity. "You wonder why I have so many prospering worlds? When I whisper to my children, I tell them they are capable of great things. I tell them they are all numbered in my heart. I tell them that love will always win in the end."

From the doorway, Aetheon watched his god die on the stone floor of the Chamber of the Gods. He watched Silveus's body turn to stardust as so many worlds had within his mighty, wrathful hands. The heavy spear sank through Silveus's ashes, the metallic tip striking the floor with a ringing clang. Aetheon turned to Narathema's watchful eye.

"Would you kill me now, God-king?" Aetheon asked.

"No, Aetheon," Narathema said. "You know it was I that spoke the seven words to your people. It was I that called you to greatness. You have earned your seat at a table of creation." Narathema gestured to Silveus's empty desk nearby. "Will you now do what your creator could not?"

Aetheon walked past the spear and took a seat at the desk. Already, Narathema could sense the power flowing into its new vessel. Narathema scooped up a handful of Silveus's ashes and walked to stand beside the table. He dumped a heap of stardust onto the wooden surface, then took Aetheon's hand and dipped it into the bowl of Lifewater. He guided his glistening fingers into the dust and watched approvingly as Aetheon began to work the clay.

A COLD EMBRACE

"Last...chance," Hiroko Yoshida said slowly, enunciating each word. I had come to know Hiroko quite well during the last three days of torture aboard the Japanese destroyer, the Makigumo.

I looked to my left at the ship's deck, at the empty spot where Ensign Aaron Winthrop had once been sitting. He hadn't made a sound when they strapped him to several heavy fuel cans and pushed him overboard. Scores of Japanese crewmembers had gathered in a wide half-circle, many scowling with arms folded across their chest. They weren't there to watch an interrogation. They wanted to see an execution. I shifted where I sat, the cords around my wrists binding me to my own weighted drum. We were somewhere in the Pacific, but the ship had been moving the entire time I was held below deck, and now endless watery horizons stretched around us in all directions. The waves were calm, and a warm sun pressed gently on my face. When I closed my eyes and ignored the bruising on my cheeks and jaw, I could almost imagine I wasn't about to die...almost.

"Hey!" Hiroko shouted and kicked my leg, returning me to reality.

Matsuji Koga, Hiroko's lead translator and part-time torturer, peeked out from behind his master. "If you don't speak on American positions, you will die like your friend."

Telling my captors the locations of sailors and soldiers would only endanger American lives, and they would kill me anyway. That much was clear to me. I lifted my chin and tried to be as defiant as Aaron had been.

"We're all gonna die one day," I smiled cynically, showing a row of bloody teeth. "You'll be right behind me." I spit a wad of red saliva onto Hiroko's right boot with a satisfying splatter.

Koga moved forward with a face full of rage, but Hiroko held up a hand that stopped him mid-step. Hiroko ignored the angry shouts from his crew, moving closer to look down on me as he blocked the sun. He nodded his head with bemused approval and flicked his chin towards the open sea behind me.

"You be brave...down there?" he asked in broken English, gesturing towards the fathoms of water I would soon be exploring.

I looked sidelong at the ship's wake in the direction where Aaron had died, and my courage fizzled out like a doused flame. I could feel my hands shaking. Hiroko noticed and smiled. He looked over his shoulder and said something in Japanese that gave his crew a great laugh. I may only speak two languages, English and broken English, but I caught the full intention of his words all the same.

Damn you, I scolded myself. *Be brave!* I ignored my own command and continued to shiver like a child left out in the cold.

"Any last words?" Koga asked, a smirk on his lips.

"Go to hell, you son of a bitch," I said, hurling the insult like a round from my Colt M1911.

Hiroko nodded as if he accepted the title, then placed a boot on my left shoulder and kicked forward with a surprising force. I cried out as I tumbled backward into the air, then remembered to suck in my final breath before I hit the water. Cold waves enveloped me in an icy grip that made me struggle not to exhale the air in my lungs. Several seconds down, and I opened my eyes, ignoring the stinging. Through a curtain of bubbles, I watched the underbelly of the Makigumo carve its way through the water, leaving me behind like discarded trash. I sank quickly as the bright sun faded and the pressure of the deep squeezed at my chest. It felt like I would sink forever, straining to free myself as I disappeared into the center of the Earth when the fuel cans struck the sea bottom. The impact forced out most of my remaining air as a sand cloud was thrown around me.

Down in the cold silence, I could feel my heartbeat drumming out a rhythm that moved through my entire body. The pain in my chest was becoming too great to withstand. *It only takes a few moments*, I told myself. *Breathe in deep and let the sea take you*. I was at war with my body, trying to deny my biological imperative to live, wanting to open my mouth, but finding I couldn't. The lack of oxygen began to trigger involuntary spasms in my chest and legs, and a dizzy comfort started to take over my mind. I caught a shimmering object dashing back and forth at the corner of my vision. *Was it a fish that came early to feast?* At once, a woman's pale, beautiful face appeared above me. A hallucination, no doubt, as my mind tried to calm me at the end.

The woman moved in close as cold lips pressed against mine, and I felt a rush of salty liquid project from her open mouth into mine. It overtook me, filling my lungs with a thick, bittersweet fluid. I tried to scream, but my voice was crushed beneath the water's weight. I thrashed in a panic, but my hands were still tied to the fuel drums, and my strength was spent. She drew back at arm's length, studying me, her head tilted slightly. She gave a subtle nod, a cryptic message that somehow things would be alright. I stared back at the woman, or creature, hypnotized by what I saw. The top of her body was that of a young woman, voluptuous and fair-skinned as a fresh snowfall. Her hair flowed like dark tendrils in the water, dancing across her naked chest. Two long slits ran from below each of her ears to her collarbone, accented by ridges of skin. The slits opened and closed like valves to reveal bright red filaments like the inner gills of a fish. My eyes drifted down, noting a rusted iron key around her neck, attached to a thin chain necklace. Around her navel, her body began a drastic transformation, her skin giving way to silvery blue scales that ran the length of a giant tail. It reminded me of the veil tail of the betta fish, although massive by comparison. It was long and flowing, a translucent bluish-green in a half-moon shape.

I had the startling realization I had been breathing underwater as the woman unsheathed a blade made from a shell or bone from behind her back. She began to cut my bindings when I suddenly started to choke on the seawater in my lungs. Her lips were back at mine in an instant, and the liquid from her mouth tasted sweeter than before as she replenished my lungs with the substance that somehow allowed me to breathe. She freed me and moved back as I spun around in the water, trying to get my bearings. I tried to ask how I was still alive and where she came from, but a muffled jumble of sounds was the best I could manage. She giggled as I coughed and choked on my own words. The sweet liquid she had given me was expelled during my fit, and she came to me once more, offering her lips as she breathed more life into my body. Her mouth lingered against mine, our bodies close, and I felt some stirring of desire for her that excited and terrified me.

She took my hand and propelled herself through the water, dragging me along as she moved incredibly fast. Like dark clouds in the water, schools of fish scattered and reformed behind us. Vast formations of colorful reefs passed beneath us in a blur. We began a fast ascent, the sun's light growing brighter above us, reflecting off the woman's scales in a dazzling show of color. She took me to the edge of a small island and let me go as I scrambled on hands and knees up the sandy shore.

I began to retch involuntarily, expelling the miraculous liquid in my lungs onto dry land. I found myself lying on my back, gasping for air as I stared up into a pale blue sky. I bolted upright, afraid she might have disappeared, but she was twenty feet away, weaving back and forth in the water.

"Hey!" I shouted and waved, flinching as she vanished below the surface. "No!" I cried out, stumbling back into the water. "I'm sorry, wait!".

The woman reappeared ten feet further away, watching me cautiously.

"I'm sorry," I repeated, holding my hands out, palms open. "I didn't mean to scare you. I wanted to thank you for saving my life."

She drifted closer, her head turned to the side again, caution replaced with curiosity.

"I'm James," I said, patting my chest. "What's your name?"

She would not, or could not, speak in words. Instead, when she opened her mouth, there was a sound like music, full of long, harmonizing notes, an intricate melody that conveyed emotions and conjured comforting images in my head. Her voice reminded me of several instruments playing the same part. The term was called soli.

"Soli," I said without thinking. "Can I call you Soli?"

She smiled and nodded her approval. She sang a new song that called to me, creating visions of returning to her in the water. She could have kept me down below the surface if she had wanted. She had brought me to the island to give me a choice.

My military duty demanded that I stay on the island and wait for rescue, but hadn't that same duty been the cause of my near-death experience, not an hour before? If I *had* died, all my hopes and dreams for the future would have been reduced to a folded flag passed to my parents. Life would continue, and new recruits would join to take my place. I was torn between the bitterness of that reality and the gratitude for living to see another day.

Gentle waves slapped against my legs, and Soli's song felt like a current trying to pull me out to sea. Her voice showed me the key around her neck unlocked a vast fortune deep underwater, a collection from lost wreckage of ancient explorers, traders, and pirates. Soli's voice conveyed the treasure could be mine, but she couldn't hide the longing in her melody and the desire in her heart. She turned, exposing a ridge of fins that traveled up her back to below her shoulder blades. *Sea-maid, water nymph, mermaid.* I grew up reading fairy tales, but nothing could have prepared me for meeting one in the flesh.

A distant buzzing caught my attention, and I looked up towards the sky to see two American planes weaving through the clouds. Were they looking for me? If I was spotted, would they rescue me and take me back? Would the Navy patch me up, then send me back out into the fight, back into hell? I thought about the lives I had taken in the war and the good friends I had seen die, sometimes for trivial pursuits. Then, I thought about the dark and quiet stillness of the water and the endless depths of exploration that awaited me. I watched Soli, my mystical siren and savior, a set of eyes above the water's surface. We had formed a connection I couldn't quite explain and wasn't ready to let go of. As the planes began their descent to get a clear look at the island, I made up my mind. I went to Soli, taking her hand and slipping beneath the waves as I said goodbye to the life I had once known.

THE SONS OF MERLIN

T hat man is going to die, I thought, watching Gregorio the Great tumble through the air, arms flailing. It was Saturday night at the local fairgrounds, and a giant tent had been erected for the main event. I was ten years old, and the trapeze platforms had seemed hundreds of feet in the air. Gregorio and his partner Sofia had looked like shimmering stars in their sequin-covered spandex.

The first act of their show had been mesmerizing as they flipped and spun through the air to the chorus of 'oohs and ahhs' of the crowd, myself included among them. The ringleader had stood below in the dirt circle of the tent, wearing a colorful ensemble of clothing. His jacket was deep purple with gold trim, his top hat the color of red clay. He narrated the performance with an energetic gusto, giving a play-by-play, then setting up their next death-defying move. Gregorio was about to attempt a triple somersault while Sofia caught him with her eyes blindfolded. It all sounded dangerous and thrilling, and I squeezed my dad's hand with anticipation as the dramatic beating of drums filled the arena with a joyous tension. The announcer on the radio had promised danger, but nothing like this!

Back and forth, Gregorio had swung like a pendulum, then let go as he tucked and twirled through the air. He flipped once, twice, three times, then his arms shot out like hooks, hands open, searching for Sofia's grasp. Only Sofia wasn't where

Gregorio had expected her to be. One of her guide wires slipped and dropped her trapeze bar by only a few inches, but it was enough that she was left screaming, fishing wildly in the air for Gregorio's hands. As the crowd cried in horror, Gregorio plummeted towards the hard-packed earth.

Almost every eye was turned on Gregorio. I would have watched him too if my dad hadn't tried to shield my eyes, his cupped hand forcing my gaze toward the dirt below. There was a shimmering of light about a foot or two off the ground, and a blurry distortion in the air, like heat waves rising off the asphalt in the summer. Further back, I saw the ringmaster holding what I thought had been a cheap novelty wand, his brows locked with furious concentration. He was crouched behind a section of the bleachers, further concealing himself from detection. Gregorio's body hit the invisible waves like a belly flop into water, his arms and legs shooting out as he came to an immediate and suspended halt. The cries and shrieks of the spectators were cut off and replaced with a collective gasp.

The ringmaster hurried forward, clapping and smiling dramatically, giving some pretense that everything had been a mere stunt, some trick of light and clear wire. Gregorio looked just as surprised as the rest of us, the color gone from his face. The ringmaster whispered something into his ear, and his shell-shocked mask slowly shifted into an unsteady smile. The crowd was slowly won over with the help of the other circus performers, adding their enthusiastic shouting and clapping to sell the illusion and coax the onlookers back into good spirits. I was disappointed to see my father clapping and slowly shaking his head.

"Dad!" I shouted over the clamor all around us. "Dad, did you see that?" I asked, pointing to where the invisible cushion of air had been.

"Oh, I saw it!" my dad said, ruffling my hair and smiling.

I frowned. Dad hadn't seen the real magic at all. I knew then that no matter how I tried to explain what had *really* happened, he would only think my mind had played tricks on me.

Eventually, he might humor me to get me to drop it, but there was nothing I could say to make him believe me.

"That's all for tonight, folks," the ringmaster said, speaking into a small handheld microphone. "If you like what you saw tonight, remember to drop a tip in the collection bins on your way out!"

There was a large stirring in the crowd as many guests stood to leave.

"Come on, Paul," my father said, standing. "If we hurry, we can try to beat some of the traffic."

I left that night feeling mystified and a little bit cheated somehow. The ringmaster had used *real* magic, but only once. What other wonders might he be able to perform? It made everything else I had seen that night seem cheap by comparison.

On our way out of the big top tent, my dad tossed a buck into one of the bins by the door, guarded by a smiling clown with large biceps. I had the feeling that if someone were to reach too far down into the bin, the clown's grin would quickly vanish, and those arms would get a workout. I was surprised to see the ringmaster wishing the patrons a good night as dozens of folks continued to file into the fairgrounds.

"Thank you, sir," the ringmaster said to my dad as the cash left his hand.

I stopped and stared at the ringmaster, holding his gaze several feet below. He smiled warmly but absentmindedly, already turning to the next guest in line.

"I saw what you did," I said, refusing to move.

The ringmaster looked back, still looking pleasant, and said, "Wasn't it a wonderful show?"

"Your wand," I said, resisting the gentle tug of my dad's hand. "I saw what really happened. How did you do that?"

The ringmaster studied me momentarily, then squatted down to look me straight in the eyes. "Magic," he said without a hint of joking.

"Paul, let's go!" my dad said, giving me a firmer tug by the hand. "Sorry," he said, waving to a couple behind us as they waited for their turn to leave.

I let myself be led away, looking over my shoulder as I went. The ringmaster watched me go, the strangest look in his eyes. It almost seemed like he had wanted me to stay and speak with him, but my dad and I soon turned a corner, and he was gone.

The next day, I rode my bike to the edge of town, excited to buy another ticket for the chance to talk to the ringmaster again. My mind was brimming with questions that had come to me the night before. Who was the ringmaster? Did the magic come from that cheap wand, or was it the man holding it? What had been whispered to Gregorio after his near-death fall through the air? The shock I felt as I rounded the bend on my bike struck me like a punch to the gut. The fairgrounds were bare, stakes pulled, and tents gone. Advertisements had stated the fair would continue through the next weekend. Why had the circus left early and so abruptly? Had it been my fault? Had I spooked the ringmaster? Standing alone in the empty field, my eyes stinging with anger and disappointment, I made myself a promise. I would look for the ringmaster and his magic wand. I would find him no matter how long it took. I would be waiting much longer than a ten-year-old boy could have imagined. It would be seventeen years before I came across a small carnival performing at the World's Fair Park in Tennessee, featuring Gregorio, The Flying Rope Dancer.

I was in Knoxville, on assignment, reporting on the fortieth-anniversary celebration of the 1982 World Fair event. Street vendors and food trucks were everywhere, peddling calories and cheap memorabilia as far as the eye could see. Small-time attractions, geared mostly for children, littered the grounds, but I had heard a large tent had gone up on the Performance Lawn earlier that morning. Even now, I still love the energy of the crowds, the dozens of carnival games, and the alluring smell of freshly cooked funnel cake.

I had grown up to become a freelance travel reporter. It allowed me the flexibility to search the country, looking for stories of the unexplainable. There was a balance between paying the bills with reputable stories and veering off the acceptable paths of journalism to interview people living on the fringes of society. I've talked to basement dwellers, conspiracy theorists, the disturbed, the enlightened, and everyone in between. Ever since I was a boy, I felt there was a veil separating our world from something fantastical. Over the years, I've found a few threads worth pulling, hoping they would lead me to the threshold where the curtain would be drawn and I could finally pass over to the other side.

The sun was setting as I approached the massive tent. A golden rope stretched across the entrance with a hanging sign that read "Showtime at 6:00pm". I looked down at my watch. It read four fifteen. There was plenty of time to snoop around. I snuck around to the side and found a loose flap to wiggle beneath. Inside, long, stretching walls of PVC plastic created misshapen hallways as I made my way through a labyrinth of corridors and back rooms, searching for the ringmaster. I passed a large poster of a man in a black leotard, posing with hands on hips, the top of the poster declaring "Gregorio the Great!" in large bold letters. Some of the man's features reminded me of the Gregorio I remembered, but it wasn't the same man. I continued and emerged out the back of the large tent to a parking lot littered with small trailers and several RVs. Three small children ran past me, barefoot and laughing. Several adults and carnival workers watched me from a distance, waiting to see if I dared to enter their small community. I thought against it and walked the camp's perimeter instead, seeking the edge of the lot and searching further into a small outcropping of trees near a small lake a couple hundred yards away.

I came across a Bohemian Vargo-style wagon made from real wood decorated with beautifully elaborate designs and intricate carvings. The scrollwork was impressive, and gold leaf had been applied liberally to a variety of mythical beasts, like dragons and griffins, carved into the sloping sides of the wagon. Dozens of flowering vines worked their way upward to the roof's eaves. It was ancient, a bit gaudy, and slowly wearing down over time. Even though much of the paint was flaking off, it was still a thing of beauty and craftsmanship. It had to be where the ringmaster slept. It *had* to be.

I walked up the wooden stairs to the small front porch and firmly knocked the round door. There was no answer, so I tried the iron latch, which rattled softly but did not budge. There was a shadow that fell over me. It wasn't physical, but contained within my mind, like when you sense someone is staring at you, but more oppressive. I slowly reached into my pocket and dug my phone out, opening my camera and pressing record. My reporting instinct had established habits of documenting everything, including what felt like a potential assailant. I spun around, extending my arm like the phone was a shield. I was forcefully thrown back against the heavy wooden door by an invisible wall of force. I cried out as the air was forced from my lungs, and my phone dropped from my hand, bouncing down the front steps. Gasping for air, I saw my feet dangling several inches off the ground as the unseen pressure kept me in place.

The ringmaster stood thirty yards away, that same plastic wand pointing straight at me. He looked exactly like I had remembered him, down to the last threat of his purple jacket. He had a thin face, greasy strips of blonde hair down to his jaw, a Roman nose, and silvery blue eyes. The ringmaster lowered his arm, and there was an instant relief in my chest as I slumped back down and collapsed onto the porch. I crawled down the steps, sucking in large gulps of air as I retrieved my phone. A spiderweb of cracks wove across the screen, but the camera was still running. I stashed the phone into my pocket as the ringmaster approached, then stepped over me as he walked up the steps and casually waved the wand toward the door lock. I heard a soft hiss of metal sliding and the thump of a deadbolt receding into the door. The ringmaster opened the door, stepped halfway in, then turned back to look down at me.

"Well...are you coming?" he asked, sounding put out. With that, he slammed the door shut behind him.

I looked around, mouth open and dumbfounded, as I picked myself up and grabbed onto the stair railing to steady myself. On shaky legs, I led myself inside.

The ringmaster sat comfortably on a cushioned bench, waiting for me to join him. I sat opposite, watching his hands carefully as he still held onto his wand. He studied me silently, waiting for me to speak first.

I cleared my throat. "I was at your show the night Gregorio almost fell to his death. I saw you save him."

The ringmaster said nothing.

"I went back the next day, but you were gone," I continued. "I've been looking for you ever since."

"Well," he said, opening his hands, "Here I am. Who the hell are you?"

"I'm Paul," I said. "Paul Richardson.

"That's *some* determination, Paul," he said. "Did you want free tickets to tonight's performance? We still end the show with a trapeze act."

"Gregorio looks different," I said.

"He's the son. Gregorio Senior and Sofia are retired to a small town near Greece."

"*You* look the same," I said, looking him up and down. "How's that possible?"

"It's not so complicated," he replied coolly. "Work out, eat vegetables, get a full eight hours, use sunscreen...oh, and don't smoke."

"No," I said, annoyed by his flippancy. "You look *exactly* the same."

"Perhaps you just *think* you remember what I looked like," he said, leaning forward. "It has been seventeen years, after all. The mind forgets. The mind fills in gaps."

"Just cut the crap, alright? Ever since that night, I've been looking for you."

"Why?"

"I had to know if the magic was real."

He smirked. "And if it was, what would that even change?"

I considered his question, studying the cheap-looking wand that had performed a miracle. "I'd ask you to teach me."

"Teach you what, exactly?"

"Everything you know…about magic."

"And why would I do that?" he asked.

"You need someone you can trust. The magic, you know…it's a burden to you. Right now, you're all alone." I couldn't explain where my snap judgments and intuitions were coming from, but it all felt true as I said it. I could see my words hitting their mark by the look in his eyes. They were haunted and full of memories. He had seen much, the ringmaster, maybe too much.

"You think you know me?" he asked with a distasteful look. "Maybe you have the gift of sight, maybe not. Maybe you are just good at reading people. Most people are lonely, after all."

"After I saw you save Gregorio, I knew there was a hidden truth out there," I said. "Something *real* and *powerful*."

"And that's why you travel the country, peddling cheap tales to amuse the masses."

"Isn't that what you're doing here?" I said, motioning around like we were inside the circus.

"I'm driven by a purpose far greater than anything you could imagine," he stated.

"Tell me."

"Ignorance really is bliss, Paul. Trust me."

"If you want me to trust you, then tell me the truth," I said. "How does that wand work? What makes it special."

The ringmaster unscrewed the white cap at the end of the cheap plastic wand and set it beside him. He tilted the black tube to the side, and a thin piece of wood slid out into his other hand.

The second wand was dark and twisted in an uneven spiral, ending in a pointed tip. It looked unremarkable and menacing in its reveal like that cheap plastic sleeve had somehow contained dark forces within. Maybe my mind was just playing tricks on me but staring at the wand made an icy feeling of panic well up in my stomach.

"What's wrong with it?" I asked, standing and backing towards the door.

One of the ringmaster's eyebrows had gone up, and he looked back and forth between me and the wand.

"You can sense the curse?" he asked with surprise.

"What?" I responded. "No, I just...it feels...wrong."

"Hmm," the ringmaster replied. "Maybe fate really has brought you to me."

"Who are you, really?" I asked.

"My name is David Ambrosius," he said, spinning the wand between his fingers. "I'm the bastard son of Merlin."

◆●◆

"Merlin?" I asked dumbly. "*The* Merlin?"

"Do you know several?" David asked.

"Well, no, I guess just the one. That would mean you're—"

"Quite old," he said.

"Do you think maybe I was drawn to the wand because *I'm* a descendant of Merlin too?" I asked hopefully.

David laughed at me, and not nicely. "As a direct son of Merlin, trust that I know exactly who I've knocked up. Besides, I've been following the bloodlines throughout the years.

"How close?" I asked.

David reached to a small shelf behind his head that contained a row of thick, leatherbound ledgers. He removed one and flipped through several pages containing pictures of family trees, photographs and biographies, news clippings, and other personal information.

"Elizabeth Holt," he read aloud. "Age twenty-two, lives in

Tennessee, and possesses fractional blood ties. Shows sporadic proclivity towards magic or supernatural gifts." David closed the book and looked at me. "While I'm here in town, she will be tested." David produced a small, pointed blue gem, like a miniature obelisk, attached to a metal loop on a necklace. He let it dangle like a shrink getting ready to hypnotize a patient. The little gem seemed to rock towards me ever so slightly. David quickly stashed the stone and returned the book to the shelf.

"If this woman, Elizabeth, passed your test, what happens?" I asked.

"I will offer her the chance to become my apprentice."

"What about me? Do you think I could be sensitive to magic?" I asked.

"Absolutely not. Paul, you are quite unremarkable, my boy. You are completely ordinary," David said matter-of-factly.

It felt like a lie, but I didn't correct him. I watched his eyes scan around the inside of his wagon house. He was looking everywhere except at me.

"What happened to your dad?" I asked.

"My...*dad*?" he asked incredulously, looking at me again. "You mean the greatest wizard to ever live? The man that guided King Arthur from a child to the legend we all remember today. The man that fought in countless wars and defeated countless evils across the ages, that man?"

"Yeah, your dad," I repeated, not feeling obliged to be smitten with the old wizard. "He may have been everything you say, but he's still your dad."

My words seemed to pierce him. He stared out beyond where I sat, far into his own past.

"My father, Merlin, was a great man. But he was also a pig and a womanizer. He had a habit of taking on beautiful young women as apprentices." David's lips puckered and trembled, his left hand balled into a fist, and the knuckles turned white. "In his fashion, he took on a new apprentice named Viviene, my mother. She was well aware of his reputation, but she desired to know all his secrets...to have all his power. Back before the years of my remembering, she got the power she wanted, then betrayed him."

"Did she kill him?"

"No. The legends say after Viveiene shattered his staff, he was bound somewhere within the Broceliande Forest in France. I spent decades searching those woods, but I have found nothing."

"And your mother, what happened to her?" I asked.

"As her power grew, her love for me faded. I was abandoned on the Isle of Skye on my tenth birthday. I've heard no news of her whereabouts for several hundred years. She's the Lady of the Lake, you know."

"That's quite the pedigree, David," I confessed.

"Oh, yes," he replied.

"How many more wands are out there?"

"A good question, indeed," he replied. "Another one to consider: how many more sons and daughters did Merlin have? How soon before dark days are upon us once more?" He checked his watch and stood up. "It's almost time to begin."

"Will you take me with you?" I asked as he brushed past me and opened the door.

"You're most likely going to die along the way," he said, walking down the steps toward the tent.

I couldn't help but smile as I followed behind him. I really was looking forward to seeing the show.

FURY ON THE WATER

Collin Drake rolled onto his back, panting, a vague smile playing at the corners of his mouth. Elena lay beside him, resting on her side, one hand propping her head as she looked him over.

"You're amazing," Collin said between breaths. "You know that, right?"

Elena made a show of brushing her fiery red locks over her naked shoulder.

"So, your cleaning services have met your expectations for the morning?" she asked, lips pursed in that intoxicating way only she could do.

"Exceeded!" he said as he grabbed her and pulled her onto his chest.

Collin held her close against him, savoring each moment his skin was pressed to hers. Elena was a palace maid, but he had plans to fix that situation. As third in line to the throne, Collin didn't have as much influence as his two older brothers, but he still had connections. Money could buy forged documents. A royal bloodline could be established. In a year, Elena could become a lady of the court, and in return, they would be free to marry and leave the tyrannical grasp of his father once and for all.

A series of bells rang from several decks below Collin's chambers.

"Hell's bells," Elena exclaimed, "breakfast will be over soon.

I'll be expected in the galley." She sat up straight, looking around for her uniform. She stopped, catching the disappointment in his eyes. A mischievous smile formed on her lips, and she leaned down, letting her hair drag across his face as she whispered into his ear. "Prince Drake, have you not had your breakfast?" her warm breath tickled his ear and made the hairs on his arm stand up.

"I could...eat," he grinned, his pulse quickening.

She moved on top of him, swished her hair back over her left shoulder, and giggled, biting her lip.

"I suppose I can make the time for royalty," she mused.

Collin closed his eyes and smiled, wishing he could live in that moment for the rest of his life. There was terrible crash as the door to his chamber was kicked open, wood slamming into stone, several bolts flying from the top hinge. Four guards spilled into the room, stun clubs at the ready, malice painted on their faces. Elena covered herself with one arm and fell beside Collin on the bed as he leaped up, hands raised and fists clenched tight.

"What the hell is the meaning of this!" Collin roared as the four guards shifted with anticipation.

Loud deliberate footsteps sounded in the hall as his oldest brother Marcus appeared in the shattered doorframe.

"Marcus, what are you doing?" Collin demanded, hands shaking from the sudden rush of adrenaline.

Marcus swept into the room, wearing his military dress uniform, complete with several rows of medals he didn't deserve, gold trim on black fabric, and a black flowing cape with a plum-colored inner lining. His ceremonial saber was attached to his hip, his boots polished mirror bright. Marcus had a dark goatee, trimmed and lined to perfection, his wavy black hair combed over and glossy with oils. Dark green eyes peered out over his sharp features, the muscles in his jaw clenching and relaxing in sharp spasms.

"Sit down, boy," Marcus sneered. "We aren't here for you; we came for the traitor."

Collin looked at Elena, then back to Marcus. "Traitor?" he

asked incredulously. "Have you lost your damn mind?"

"This is official business," Marcus continued, stepping further into the room. "If you get in my way, you *will* get hurt."

"Wait until Father hears of this!" Collin hissed, snatching his shirt from the bed, stealing a concerned look at Elena, who lay frozen in place.

"Who do you think sent me, fool? The King's Justice will be done. Take her," Marcus motioned to the guards.

Collin threw his wadded-up shirt into the face of the closest guard and followed through with a right hook that crunched into the man's nose, sending him staggering backward. Another guard came at Collin with a backhanded swing of his club. There was an explosion of pain and light as Collin was sent crashing into his nightstand, knocking over a heart-shaped music box that had been a gift from Elena. Collin had played its music often while they spent passionate nights together or let it serve as a reminder of their love when he sat alone in his quarters. It took on a new purpose as he gripped it in both hands and lunged at one of the men reaching towards Elena. There was a loud crack as the wooden heart split, along with the top of the guard's head. The man crumpled to the ground as the three remaining guards rushed at Collin. Stun clubs rained down on Collin in a blur of pain and shocks of electric current. Collin was kneeling as a club slammed into the back of his head, sending him dazed and sprawling onto the cold stone floor. His head was on fire; his vision was cloudy glass. Elena's screams were leagues away and fading further by the second. A polished black boot stepped inches from Collin's face as Marcus leaned down.

"You were warned, little brother. The King's Justice *will* be served."

Collin dreamed of years long past, running through the halls of Drake Keep, the third-largest floating castle in the world. He stood out on the bow, watching the small city cut through the water, kept afloat by a series of giant suspense discs that ran along the bottom of the vessel. His mother, Anne, was alive, standing beside him with a smile as the wind whipped loose strands of long, dark curly hair in all directions. His father, King Edward, had been kinder then, a feat Collin had owed solely to his mother. She had been their compass then, a lighthouse for the entire family as their Keep navigated uncertain tides. His mother placed a hand on his shoulder as he watched a pod of dolphins leading the hulking vessel in the water. The day she died was filled with the sound of screams and the thunderous roar of booming cannon fire as house McPherson and their hired pirates brought war to his home.

"There are rough seas ahead," she said.

He looked up and saw blood trickling from her left ear and nose, soot stains outlining her face.

Collin woke in the ship's infirmary, halfway blinded by a compress wrapped around his head. Oliver Drake, second to the throne, shook him by the shoulder. Oliver was the least cruel of Collin's family. He had once had a kind heart but eventually abandoned it in the name of self-preservation.

"Wake up, Collin, it's time!" Oliver said, thrusting a dress uniform into Collin's unsteady hands.

"For what?" Collin asked, thoroughly confused.

"Elena's execution. She's walking the plank."

The plank was a mechanical platform at the top of the fifty-deck Keep. A prisoner sentenced to death stood on the platform, bound, as an anchor was tied to their feet. A simple engraved plaque was attached to the anchor, stating their crime for Davy Jones to read below. They were given last words, then the platform extended thirty feet over the water. At the King's signal, a trap door beneath the prisoner's feet dropped, and the unfortunate soul rushed to meet a watery grave.

Collin stood in the King's viewing box on the main deck, holding onto the polished railing to keep from falling over, his head swimming and knees still weak. Elena stood out on the extended platform, head shaved and arms bound behind her back as the King's orator read off her crimes into a speaker system. The decks were lined with spectators, some sneering, but most stood by idly.

"...pirate, conspirator, traitor," the orator bellowed with contempt.

Elena watched the King with her head held high, a shocking amount of defiance chiseled into her face. *How long had he been unconscious?* Collin tried to think. *He had to stop this!*

"Father, I..." Collin faltered.

King Edward made a subtle shift from one foot to the other, his eyes cutting down upon Collin for a fraction of a second, then to Marcus. Marcus took a stiff, formal sidestep to appear behind Collin.

"Unless you'd like to join her, keep your damn mouth shut," he hissed. "Third to the throne will not be missed."

"I..." Collin couldn't find the words. A cold panic had gripped him, squeezing his throat, crushing his chest. *What could he do? There was nothing he could do!*

"Do you have any last words?" the orator's voice boomed.

"Today, the empire reigns through fear and violence, but this will not last," Elena shouted, her voice picking up and carrying across the speakers. "One day, the people will rise up. They need only listen to the music in their heart to guide them. The heart will steer you. The light is sealed with a kiss."

Elena looked towards the King's box, and her watery eyes fell on Collin. "It was always real. Always."

The trapdoor below Elena's feet dropped, and she was gone, pulled down towards the water with alarming speed. The anchor hit the water's surface with a slap, sending up a plume of spray that swallowed Elena whole. Collin felt strong arms pulling at him and realized he had been trying to climb over the railing. Two guards dragged him to a staircase entrance right behind the grandstand seating, promising violence as they went.

———————●●●———————

Collin lay on the floor for several hours, brimming with shame and grief, aching all over from the beating he had received in his doorway. *He could have done more; he should have done more!* Collin slowly rolled over, noticing his night lantern resting on its side beneath the bed, thankfully unbroken in the scuffle. He slowly set himself and the lantern right side up and reignited the flame. A faint outline of lipstick brightened on the ring of the glass, a kiss mark Elena had playfully warned him never to wipe away as proof of her love.

The music box lay in two pieces on his mattress, speckled in blood. Collin held the two halves of the wooden heart in his hands, dragging his fingers slowly across the inside of the shell's pockmarked surface. There were odd imperfections, deliberately etched in, undetectable from the outside. Elena's final words haunted him, a cryptic message he knew had been meant for him alone. *The heart. The light.* He held the heart together and set it gently, point facing down, into the top of the lantern. The light within caused a message to appear:

'God save thee, ancient Mariner!
From the fiends, that plague thee thus!—
Why look'st thou so?'—With my cross-bow
I shot the albatross.
25.0000° N, 71.0000° W

The Rime of the Ancient Mariner. It was an ancient poem, now in the form of a clue. Elena was speaking to him from beyond the grave, guiding him, but to where? This woman he loved, who had she really been? Collin went to the hearth, poured the lantern oil onto the wooden heart, and set it aflame. If Elena had been a rebel, his path would now be a dangerous one. Keep Drake would be docking at the New Francisco islands in several weeks. When they did, he would find his moment to slip away. Until then, he would keep up appearances. He pulled his polished saber and scabbard from his wardrobe, wrapped the belt tightly around his waist, and straightened his golden buckle. He would find the rebels. He would convince them to help him. He would avenge Elena. *Everyone* responsible was going to pay. An impossible notion formed in his mind, pulling on him like a rough current. Somehow, someway, he was going to kill his father. He was going to kill the King

SEMPITERNAL

The stink of burning wreckage filled Henry Claremont's nose as an acute pain in his leg brought him back to consciousness. His crewmate, Robert Lewis, was tightening a bloody bandage around one of Henry's outstretched legs, using his TL-122 flashlight tucked beneath his armpit to see in the dark.

"Ah, steady!" Henry groaned as Robert cinched down the fabric in place.

"Don't snap your cap," Robert replied calmly. Robert's forehead and cheeks were smudged, filthy with dirt and what might be engine grease or blood; Henry couldn't distinguish which. Robert examined his work with a slight nod of approval.

"You'll live, Henry," he said slumping back against the muddy wall of a trench.

"How did we get here?" Henry asked, his last clear memory being 30,000 feet off the ground inside the B-17 he and Robert was assigned as gunners.

"Well, Sergeant," Robert said with a smirk, "Would you like to start with getting shot down by the krauts or after we crashed in the sticks and I dragged your heavy ass across two fields to this trench?"

Henry tried to sit up straight, but a searing pain in his leg quickly pulled him back to the damp ground.

"The crew?" he asked, breathing heavily.

"Dead," Robert said grimly. "I recovered Jim's service pistol, a few sticks of beef jerky, a canteen of water, and those bandages," he said, pointing to his leg.

"How bad is it?" Henry asked, nodding at a long red stain running from his knee almost to his ankle. "There's not much pain."

"Just wait until the endorphins wear off..." Robert said.

"Give it to me straight, Bob!" Henry demanded.

"Your landing gear is busted, Henry-boy," he replied. "I doubt you can stand, let alone walk."

Henry stared at his ruined leg, thinking back on his combat crew transition training and the instructor that had set the entire class on pins and needles as he quoted survival rates for aircrews that got shot down behind enemy lines. As a gunner, Henry's job was to ensure this exact scenario didn't happen, and he had failed miserably. Henry had done well enough at operating radios at the schoolhouse, but the combat part had been a constant struggle. It had been Robert who had helped him through the training. Robert had been something of a prodigy, and God knows why he had chosen to take Henry under his wing. The rest of the class had been jealous of him, but he and Henry had fallen in together, becoming thick as thieves along the way. Now, Henry considered their odds of survival and knew one variable was shooting their chances straight to hell; him.

"Well then," Henry said, raising his chin proudly. "You know what you have to do."

Robert stared at him, his eyebrows drooping lower and lower with disapproval. "And what would that be?" he asked at last.

"You've got to leave me here," Henry said, wincing. "You've got to get yourself to safety. Try to meet up with French resistance and make your way to Switzerland. You still have a chance!"

Robert smiled kindly and shook his head side to side as he cut off the flashlight, leaned back against his side of the trench wall, and stared at a full moon. He spun a thick golden ring on his left hand, using his thumb and pinky to work the metal in a circle. Henry heard a faint popping sound of machine gun fire in the distance. With only one handgun between them, if the Germans came over the crest of dirt, things would go belly up fast.

"I think I'll stay a bit," Robert said casually. "You were always great for conversation. You'd be surprised how hard that can be to find." He rubbed his ring with his thumb.

"You've got a girl back home," Henry protested, referring to the ring. "I always thought it strange you never talked about her, but I figured some men like their lives private."

Robert kept smiling as he held up the ring, catching slivers of moonlight. "I'm not married," he said. "At least I haven't been for a long time."

"Oh, sorry," Henry said. "I just figured..."

"Don't sweat it," Robert said. "In fact, did you know that wearing a ring on this particular finger," and he tapped his ring finger, "wasn't even a thing if you go back several thousand years. Maybe I should have picked the pointer finger or this one." Robert shot a middle finger in the direction of their downed plane.

What do you mean, picked?" Henry asked with a confused chuckle.

"Henry, I've been watching you these last ten missions we've flown," he replied, ignoring the question. "I never fit in with the rest of the crew, but you've always had my back, don't think I didn't notice."

"What are friends for?" Henry mused, looking down at his bandages, noting a troubling amount of red. "I'll tell you what, if the Nazis don't get us, I'll buy you a cold beer when we get back."

"Make it a Guinness; I'm partial to them," Robert said, looking Henry over with an appraising stare. "They might not let you drink with that baby face, though."

"I'm twenty-three, same as you," Henry replied.

"Huh?" Robert looked genuinely confused.

"Twenty-three, cabbage head," Henry teased. "You told me we were the same age when we first met."

Robert snapped his fingers and gave a mock 'tsk tsk' with his pointer finger. "Right you are, Henry, right you are."

There was a loud explosion several hundred yards away, and Henry felt the vibrations through the dirt, followed by inaudible shouting and more gunfire.

"Getting close now," Robert observed. "Tell me something, Henry, what would you do if you could live forever?"

"What?" Henry asked, dumbfounded. His heart was pounding, and it felt like a ball of ice was sitting in his stomach.

"What would you do if you could live forever," Robert asked again, speaking slowly, as if he had all the time in the world.

"Robert, you don't have time for this; you need to go now!" Henry shouted, feeling a flash of anger towards Robert for having the means to escape yet choosing not to take it.

"No!" Robert snapped. "I want to know; it's important."

"There's no time!" Henry hissed, gripping his leg as he felt a fresh stab of pain.

"Just tell me, and I'll go," Robert replied.

Henry could see he wasn't going to budge. He would have to humor him if he wanted to save his bull-headed friend.

"I suppose," Henry began, "I would see the world."

"Meh," Robert said, rocking his outstretched palm from side to side.

"All of it!" Henry added. "Every square inch! Even the oceans!"

"Better," Robert smiled.

"Who knows, maybe even one day, up there," Henry pointed to a cluster of twinkling stars high in the sky.

When he looked back down, Robert was staring at him intently, two points of reflected moonlight in his eyes.

"And when you've explored it all, or as much as you care to, then what?" Robert asked, a hint of bitterness in his voice.

"I don't know, maybe settle down, try to find love," Henry offered, trying to scan the top of the trench in the darkness.

"And when the people you love have all grown old and died, and you've loved again and lost again so many times that their names and faces all run together, then what?"

"Jesus, Bob," Henry said, looking back. "I hadn't even considered that."

"Well, consider it now," Robert said flatly.

There was a fresh round of gunfire exchange as tracer rounds zipped overhead, pressing Henry hard into the packed earth. There was more shouting, closer now. Robert sat motionless, spinning his ring and watching Henry.

"Consider it," he said again, almost in a whisper. "Would you seek out death, knowing that this physical life held no more surprises?"

Henry didn't want to dwell on such morbid thoughts, but he couldn't shake how Robert looked at him. There was an eagerness to hear Henry's responses, a severe focus of Robert's attention. Henry figured it was better to die speaking with a friend than crawling through the mud like an injured dog, only to get a bullet or knife in the back.

"I'd look for others," Henry said. "Others that live forever. I'd form a group, and we'd make decisions together. I'd figure out why we were given our gift. I'd discover our true purpose."

Robert nodded slowly, then rose to his feet.

"Are you sauced? Get down!" Henry shouted.

"There isn't much time, Henry. I need you to listen and listen well," Robert said, producing their deceased pilot's service pistol. "I can try to explain things until I'm blue in the face, which will take a long time, believe me. Or I can just show you and get that first shock out of the way."

"Bob, what in the he—"

Robert placed the pistol beneath his chin and pulled the trigger. The shot was deafening, amplified by the trench walls, setting Henry's ears to ring at once. Henry cried out in horror, expecting to see the top of Bob's head popping off like a Fourth of July firework, but instead, the man sat on his haunches, alive and unharmed. Henry looked wide-eyed at a small impacted bullet that had dropped between his feet, the tip of lead blossoming like a smashed flower.

"Impossible," Henry managed weakly.

"Even impossible has its limits," Robert replied, placing his right thumb and forefinger around his ring. "I want you to find the others…if they even exist. See the world and find the others."

"But you…you…" Henry's head was spinning.

"I'm very tired, Henry," he said. "The things I've seen," Robert said, staring through Henry to some distant memory. "I'm ready for my next adventure, and it lies beyond this life."

The shouting of German soldiers could be heard no more than thirty yards away.

"I wish there was more time," Robert said regretfully. "I wish I could explain things...guide you. I want you to promise me something. No matter what happens, you don't surrender. Do you understand me?"

"But my leg, I—"

"Promise me!" Robert shouted, making Henry flinch.

"I promise," Henry said solemnly.

"You keep fighting and keep moving," Robert said with a quick grimace as he slipped his ring over the knuckle and off his hand. He quickly transferred the ring onto Henry's left pointer finger. "Miles to go before you sleep," he smiled. Robert's face suddenly went slack. "Oh," he said with a mix of wonder and surprise. His knees buckled, and he toppled sideways into the dirt, the gun spilling from his hand.

Henry stared at Robert's lifeless body in disbelief, then looked at the golden ring adorning his finger, shimmering in the full moon's light. A rush of adrenaline hit Henry, taking his breath as if he had jumped into a pool of ice water. The throbbing in his leg vanished, erased, the entire idea of pain seemed foreign. A burst of energy moved through his entire body, like sunlight had been injected straight into his veins, and he sprang to his feet, taking in several exhilarated breaths. He leaned down and picked up the pistol, looking up in time to see a half dozen German soldiers appear at the top of the trench, shining flashlights and pointing their Karabiner rifles as they screamed orders in broken English. Henry stared back, feeling his fears melt away, evaporating into the cool night air.

"I'm sorry," he said, rubbing the golden ring with his thumb. "But I made a promise." He looked down toward Robert, but there was only a flattened gunner's uniform, motes of dust blowing out the collar and sleeves. "And I intend to keep it,"

Henry said. He raised the pistol and started to fire.

II. HORROR

"Horror is like a serpent; always shedding its skin, always changing. And it will always come back." -Dario Argento

RAVEN HOUSE

"**S**pirit of the Raven, hear my call!"

Pit...pat...pat. Three drops of Maggie's blood fell onto the offering plate of the raven statue, which seemed to glow silver in the moonlight. The statue was roughly the size of a real raven, though this one had its wings spread dramatically. The circular dish at its feet had perhaps once been used to hold a candle or glass orb. Now it served as an offering plate, ready to accept payment.

The room was cold from the holes in the roof and cracks in the plaster of the walls. Several windows were shattered, but they still let in enough light on a full moon to see. Even so, the girls brought battery-powered lanterns, painting the room in artificial fluorescence and plunging areas beyond the light into deeper shadow.

Maggie turned to her younger cousin Tessa and her two friends, Kiren and Jackie. The girls were about to be freshmen in high school, while Maggie was already heading into her senior year. Soon enough, she would be off to college in Boston, free of her tag-a-longs and the dreary boredom of their sleepy New England town.

She had brought Tessa and her friends to Raven House, an abandoned Victorian-style home set back in the woods on the outskirts of town. It was a long-standing tradition for the high school seniors to bring freshmen to Raven House, tell them the haunted tale, and bind the group of impressionable young teenagers together in fear and excitement. Maggie had participated in the same ritual when she was Tessa's age. For almost two years, she had returned to Raven House on the nights of a full moon with her friends, offering drops of blood to the raven and asking for good fortune or a passing grade on an upcoming exam. Eventually, the magic faded, as all things do. Maggie grew up and moved on, but in her heart, she still longed for that rush of excitement when a drop of blood hit the offering plate, and she truly believed anything might be possible. That's why she returned and passed on the tale to the younger girls. It was her way of staying connected to the story and a little piece of the magic. Once she left for college, she wouldn't have time for any more childish games.

Maggie stood tall before the statue on the fireplace mantle while the three younger girls sat at the decrepit dining room table, positioned several feet away.

"There have been many rumors over the years about what happened in this house, but the locals know the real story and have passed it down through the generations," Maggie said, looking over their awestruck faces. "There once was a wealthy man and woman who lived in the house around fifty years ago. The man was often away on business, and his beautiful bride grew lonely and decided to take a lover while he was gone. During one of the man's business trips, he had come home early, hoping to surprise his wife with a gift he had acquired on his travels. The raven statue would be the last gift he ever bought."

"He caught them, didn't he?" asked Tessa.

"Obviously," Kiren said, rolling her eyes.

"Of course, he found his wife and her lover in the bed, and of course, he flew into a violent rage!" Maggie declared, recapturing their attention. "But instead of killing them both, he slit his wrists and bled out while holding out the raven statue, vowing to find his true love in the next life!"

"Then what happened?" Tessa asked eagerly.

"The wife, stricken with guilt, kept the statue, placing it on the mantle for many years. Every night, she would pray to the raven, begging the ghost of her husband for forgiveness. As her inheritance began to dwindle, she prayed to her dead husband to save her from becoming destitute," Maggie said.

"That means poor," Kiren said, shouldering Jackie.

Maggie moved in close. The wooden table was stained and rotting, chipped and abused like everything else in Raven House. "Eventually, she started to prick her finger and offer drops of her blood as a sacrifice." Maggie held up her bloody pointer finger. "Then, one day, she awoke the next morning to find a tiny little chest sitting on the table, right there!" The girls shifted around nervously.

The walls creaked and groaned as the wind picked up and pressed firmly into the sides of the house.

"So, the wife was saved?" asked Jackie.

"Doubtful," Kiren added.

"The wife opened the box to find it was full of bloody silver coins. Before she could take them, the raven came alive and flew at her, pecking out her eyes!"

Maggie pulled down the skin beneath her own eyes, looking to the ceiling to show the whites of her eyeballs, smearing a drop of blood on her face in the process. Tessa and Jackie were on edge. Kiren was at least entertained.

"After that, the woman went insane," Maggie said. "They shipped her off to a mental institution, and she was never heard from again. Now, up with you."

Maggie took out a small sewing kit and passed each of them a small needle. "Now remember," she said. "Prick your finger, give your sacrifice, then make your wish. If the raven finds you worthy, he will deliver your request at a time of his choosing."

"What if you're not worthy?" Tessa asked nervously.

"Well then, he might just fly to your bedroom and peck out your eyes!" Maggie shrieked.

They all allowed themselves a laugh, then made their way to the statue on the mantle one by one.

When it was Tessa's turn, she stood anxiously before the raven, picking at her fingernails.

"What's wrong?" Maggie asked.

"I want to ask, but I'm scared of what could happen," Tessa

said. "I don't want to hurt anyone."

"Why don't you whisper it to me, and I'll ask for you," Maggie offered.

Tessa's hushed voice told her about a girl at school, Eliza Billings, that had been bullying Tessa all year. She was the vice principal's kid, so many of the teachers were scared to punish her.

"You don't need a wish for me to kick her ass," Maggie said angrily. "I just wish you had told me before."

Maggie took Tessa's needle and pricked her own middle finger. She dropped three more drops of blood into the small dish.

"I've got you," Maggie winked.

"Oh, raven," Maggie cried out dramatically. "Please help Tessa get rid of her tormentor. Stop Eliza Billings and teach her a lesson!"

Tessa gave a devilish grin of approval. Maggie led the girls out of Raven House, laughing and in high spirits, a trail of lanterns piercing the black veil of night.

———————◆●●◆———————

Three days later, Maggie received a frantic call from Tessa, demanding they meet immediately. Several blocks from Tessa's house, Maggie drove to the local park and found her on a wooden bench, looking like she hadn't slept, with dark rings forming beneath a haunted stare.

"Jesus, Tessa, what's going on?" Maggie asked, rushing to sit by her side.

"We did something terrible, Maggie!" she cried. "It's all my fault!"

"What is it? Tell me!" Maggie said, feeling her own heart start to race.

"The wish," Tessa said. "We made a horrible wish."

Maggie felt a rush of relief. She smiled and wrapped Tessa up in a tight hug. "Oh, Tessa, you scared me! The wishes are just for fun. It's like a fortune cookie."

Tessa pushed Maggie back so she could look into her eyes. "You don't get it, Maggie. You wished something bad would happen to Eliza."

"And?" Maggie asked.

"She's gone missing!" Tessa said. "A police officer stopped by our class and was asking questions! We have to go back to Raven House," she insisted. "We have to take back the wish!"

"I'm sure it's a coincidence," Maggie assured her. "Maybe she ran away or something."

"We did this!" Tessa yelled, "You have to help me fix it, please!"

Maggie knew the raven was plastic, painted to look like metal. Over the years, the raven had been broken or stolen many times. Maggie hoped when Tessa saw and held the plastic bird, it would snap her out of her hysteria.

"I'll take you there, but just to show you, it's not real!" Maggie said.

It was almost a forty-minute drive to get back to Raven House. They entered the house in silence as beams of sunlight stabbed through the crumbling walls and ceiling, illuminating the rotting structure and dispelling its shadowy intrigue from the night of the blood ritual. As their footfalls echoed inside the empty house, Maggie smelled the putrid aroma only moments before she marched Tessa into the dining room. Tessa's pained shrieking amplified inside the open space, making Maggie's ears ring. Although she had never met Eliza, Maggie was sure it was her dead body lying on the kitchen table, her skin a sickly blueish purple. The raven statue sat perched on the mantle; wings proudly displayed as it watched in silent accusation. There was a heavy thud beside Maggie as Tessa's body hit the floor.

"It's not real," Maggie whispered to the raven, feeling her knees tremble. "It's just a story; it's not real!" She felt tears welling up in her eyes.

Maggie took Tessa by the wrists and dragged her back toward the door. Haunted or not, a girl was dead in the house, and they had to go to the police.

"It's not real," Maggie said to herself, repeatedly, struggling to pull Tessa across the floor. "It's not real!"

"It's real to me," a gravelly voice said from behind Maggie.

Maggie screamed and dropped Tessa's hands, whirling around to see a looming male figure blocking the door. The man was weathered and dirty as the wooden planks beneath his bare feet. He was dressed in stained hospital scrubs and wore a patient intake band clasped around his wrist. There was a wild brightness to his eyes, both magical and deadly.

"Who...who are y...you?" Maggie stammered.

"I am the Raven," the man said, his chin raised proudly. "I heard your wish and accepted your payment in blood."

"I didn't want this!" Maggie shouted. "How did you even..." she trailed off as a sick realization came. "You were in the house the whole time, listening."

"The Raven went out and found the girl," he said. "The Raven made your wish come true."

"What does the Raven want now?" Maggie asked, keeping herself between Tessa's unconscious body and the man.

"I'm still bound to this house," he said, "but this body is only temporary. His mind is too weak. I need a strong host."

Maggie let out a yelp as the man's body went rigid, and his eyes rolled back in his head. His mouth fell open, and a blurry shape, writhing and folding in the air, shot out and passed into her body. She clutched her chest at the freezing chill that overtook her, sending her to her knees. The man had crumpled into a pile on the ground, appearing lifeless. A scratching sound came from behind Maggie, making her turn slowly as she fought to pull breath into her lungs. No longer a statue, the raven drew in its wings and let out a gurgling croak that filled Maggie's head with a cacophony of raspy calls, echoing and bouncing around inside her mind, drowning out her thoughts.

She could feel her willpower draining away, replaced by a desire to serve the spirit of the Raven King. He did not grant wishes to bring fulfillment to others; he had merely been looking for a suitable host. Within Maggie, he had found a worthy servant. Her last fleeting thought was that there was no escape. She was now a part of Raven House.

HELL RETRIEVAL DIVISION

B rother Psalm's eyes fell upon our small group of initiates. He was tall and imposing, hands clasped behind his spotless white robes. His head was shaved smooth, reflecting firelight off the top of his scalp, casting shadows across his eyes so that the sockets almost looked empty.

"Later tonight," Brother Psalm began, his voice loud and full of bass, "far below Saint Peter's Basilica, past the lowest known levels of The Tomb of the Dead, our team will enter Hell. God willing, we will find the soul of Jillian Vickers, exercise her spirit to Heaven, and return through the portal with all ten of our members alive and intact. We are the Hell Retrieval Division and go where no other dares to tread!"

We had been preparing for this day for nine months, but hearing his words made the hairs on my neck and arms stand up. In the back of my mind, I always thought of the Hell Gate as some abstract idea or metaphor. *Within all men lies a gateway to Hell.* The two other initiates, Deacons Shaw and Kent, exchanged nervous glances but nodded their willingness to continue. I gave a grim nod, unsure if I had just agreed to damnation, and rose to join them.

We were joined by five other priests, Brothers Job, Amos, Hosea, Micah, and Ezra. A sixth member, a woman known as Leviticus, fell in line as Brother Psalm unlocked the heavy wooden door leading to the Vatican Necropolis. Down we went, level after level until the air felt thick as soup in the dark and winding staircase. The only light came from torches held by the line of seven robed figures preceding me. There was a heavy smell of damp mold from centuries of moisture trapped within the smooth stone.

"Why's there a woman here?" Shaw whispered to Kent. "She can't be a priest."

"She's not!" Brother Ezra's voice bounced off the tight stone corridor. "Now keep your thoughts in your head and hold your tongue, Deacon Shaw."

"Yes, Brother Ezra," Shaw answered obediently.

After what might have been ten more minutes of descending, the air became dry and stale. The steps abruptly stopped as the stairwell opened into a large chamber shaped like a hollowed-out cathedral, with the Hell Gate positioned directly in the center of the floor. The seven torches were used to light sconces, candles, and more lighting fixtures. The walls and ceiling did not merely reflect the shape of a church but the composition as well. Crosses and images of Christ had been affixed in excessive numbers along the walls. There were statues, carvings of angels, and paintings depicting God's glory and the smiting of demons. It was all quite gaudy, feeling more like the superstitious precautions of the overzealous than holy wards to danger. The Hell Gate itself was a stone circle, maybe ten feet across. The stone was divided into six equal pieces, each covered in carved lines that reminded me of Celtic knots. A small trough ran around the entire gate, with heavy stone handles sticking from the ground at intervals corresponding with one of the six pieces of the stone door that lay flat on the floor.

"Wait here," Brother Psalm said abruptly as he and the five other priests each took a position at one of the stone handles, leaving Leviticus and us to observe from fifteen paces away.

"During the ceremony, things will be much different," Brother Psalm said. "There will be more priests, as well as the Pope."

"The Pope!" I barked stupidly.

The other five priests stared at me like I was a bit slow, while

Brother Psalm slowly nodded his head without adding a further explanation.

"Ready," Brother Psalm began, addressing his fellow priests. "Begin."

The six ordained priests began to push on their assigned handles with a visible strain. The veins stood out at Brother Psalm's temples, and he gritted his teeth as his face grew flush in the uneven lighting. For men in their late fifties, they all appeared in excellent shape. There was a sound like an ancient tree trunk cracking and splitting as the six stone pieces parted and began withdrawing back into a track beneath the surrounding stone floor. I held my breath, half expecting flames to shoot up from the floor, but as the stones came to rest inside their compartments, all was quiet, and the room's temperature even felt like it had dropped several degrees. The priests stood quietly, hands resting on the stone handles of the gate mechanism as Brother Psalm motioned me towards the open portal, then replaced his hands before him. I crept forward cautiously, my mind racing at the possibilities of what could be just beyond the lip of the gaping ring in the floor. To my surprise, the hole was full of murky water ten feet down. A stone staircase, cracked and in disrepair, led down and into the water, continuing below the surface until the outline of the steps disappeared into darkness. Leviticus had followed and stood several paces behind me; her eyes closed as she held up one hand as if commanding an unseen presence to halt.

"How far does it go?" I heard myself asking.

"Many fathoms," Brother Psalm said. "But this is not the way to Hell."

He looked around at the other priests, and an understanding passed between them. In unison, they moved to the other side of the door handles and pushed with force once more until the six pieces met with a thud, sealing the stone portal.

"There is a ritual," Brother Psalm said, breathing heavily, "that will open the gateway." He came close to me, looking grim. "The next time those doors open, it won't be water that you see."

My tongue felt swollen and tasted sour as I tried to swallow.

"It's time to head back," Brother Amos spoke up. "We've still got preparations for tonight."

I watched Leviticus join the men and head back towards the staircase as Brother Psalm watched Kent, Shaw, and I over the weak flickers of his solitary torch. There was something off-putting about the silent woman. She had dark hair, pulled back and bound tightly, with sharp lines in her face and a predatory stare.

"Who is she, Brother Psalm?" I asked.

"Levi is...unique to the team," Brother Psalm said, carefully parceling out his words. "She is necessary for locating our quarry. She has certain abilities for communing in the spiritual realm."

"She's a medium?" Kent guessed.

"That is a word for it, yes," Brother Psalm said.

"A man or a woman who is a medium or a necromancer shall surely be put to death," Shaw quoted from scripture.

"Where better to use an ability from the Devil than in the realm of the beast," Brother Psalm offered. "Levi is the only one who can locate the spirit of Jillian Vickers. Hell is vast, Deacon Shaw. Far more than you could ever imagine."

"How does she find the people we seek?" Kent asked.

"She uses the personal belongings of the deceased to form a connection," Brother Psalm said. "It's like a tether between the living and the dead. She follows the string, and we find our target at the other end."

"We didn't open the portal just now," I said, remembering how she seemed to stand guard. "What was she doing then?"

"She was communing," Brother Psalm said. "And making sure nothing tried to sneak through from the other side. "*Any* time that hole opens up, there is a risk."

It made sense in a way, using a psychic to find a spirit, but the hypocrisy of it stung. Other questions crept up as if a separate gate had been opened in my mind.

Brother Psalm looked at me, and I could tell he was waiting

for my next question.

"Brother Psalm, why would someone retrieve souls from Hell in the first place? Wouldn't the trapped soul be there for a reason?" I asked.

"To answer the second question, yes, they were judged and sent to Hell to join the ever-growing ranks of sinners. As to why we risk everything to traverse the chaotic dimension of the damned..." he trailed off. "It's important if you think of the church as a business. Doing the Lord's work takes capital. The millionaires and billionaires of the world have plenty, and they are more than willing to pay to ensure a one-way ticket to the kingdom of God."

I couldn't believe what I heard, even standing beside a 'Hell Gate'. How could the church try to circumvent the will of God for money?

"Deacon Russo, did you know that the Catholic Church is the largest private provider of educational and medical assistance in the world? Where do you think that money comes from? The average person donates, but it's a drop in the bucket to what we truly need to accomplish our charitable works and advance the kingdom of Heaven."

"Brother Psalm, how can we go against the will of God, then expect him to offer us his protection?"

"It's our faith that allows us to access this portal. Why would God allow us this pathway if He was not with us? Would He not punish us instead?"

"Who says he still won't?" I asked.

Brother Psalm ignored me, turned, and led the way back up the winding stairs, forcing Shaw, Kent, and me to follow or remain in the dark. He said nothing as we walked, and I found my thoughts drifting back nine months prior. There were eighteen deacons to volunteer to join the secret offshoot of the officially recognized priesthood within the Vatican. After an extensive screening process, we had gone down to ten. The psychological trials had reduced us to five. Back then, Father Marlo, also known as Father Morpheus, had begun psychological training with a question.

"How does one prepare for Hell?" he had asked my group back in the fall of 1994.

As we looked on dumbly, Father Marlo had reached into his robes and removed a single mushroom, holding it up to the light. It had a small red umbrella cap dotted white with smooth gills underneath and a thick white stem. While I had never taken drugs up to that point, my father lived through the 70s. He had recounted cautionary tales of friends and acquaintances taking psychedelics, sometimes to disastrous effects.

"To fathom Hell or soar angelic, just take a pinch of psychedelic. Dr. Humphry Osmond," Father Marlo quoted.

"Will we be eating those?" I had found myself asking aloud to the sound of a few nervous laughs.

"Mental fortitude is a skill," Father Marlo said without a hint of amusement. "Skills can be learned; technique can be taught. To harden the mind is akin to hardening the body. It takes repetition and practice."

To my bewilderment, Father Marlo popped the mushroom into his mouth and began to chew. He took a white drawstring bag from his robe and began to walk around the room, taking out additional mushrooms like the one he had just consumed and putting them in front of each initiate, myself included.

"I ask you to walk a dangerous path now, but know I have walked it myself."

He stood, silently watching us. His face showed no feelings of hostility or expectancy. If anything, he had an air of curiosity about him, as if he were about to embark on a leisurely Sunday drive and wanted to know who might be joining him. We all ate our mushrooms.

Apart from some initial stomach pains, the overall experience had been exhilarating and spiritually significant. The patterns on the walls and floors had shifted in swirling spirals, air currents moved like water, and colors became more vibrant than I had thought possible. I felt the warmth of God shining through like a beam of living sunlight. That had been our first experience, but not the last. Many of our future sessions would hold no joy.

During the mind trials that followed, our session leaders took things to an extreme that bordered on criminal abuse, akin to psychological torture. The lights of the Vatican catacombs were set to flicker and flash in a disjointed rhythm, alternating between painful bright and pitch black. Masked men, presumably other priests, were brought in to scream, shout, and threaten, tearing at clothing covered in fake blood. The rooms would be full of prompts and triggers to induce what some call a "bad trip". I learned back then the mind can be a powerful weapon, especially when turned against its owner, but I also learned how to endure the pains of the mind and how to create barriers against attack.

I thought about those times, filled with elation and misery, as I ascended the stairs in silence behind Brother Psalm. Hell Retrieval Division priests were named after holy books from the bible to protect their true names, although it seemed like superstition to me. Members of the HRD were required to retire after their seventh journey to Hell. Tonight, I would follow the priests into Hell as an observer. During the next mission, Brother Psalm's final mission, one the initiates would lead, and Brother Psalm would follow. After that, one of the initiates would become the next Brother Psalm.

———————◆●◗———————

That night, I found myself back in the underground cathedral, but our procession had swelled in numbers, for the ritual to open the gate required more men, including Pope John Paul II. While the complete entourage of the Pope was not invited to the event, a handful of Cardinals and Retrieval Division hopefuls were in attendance. There was also a small company of the Pope's personal guard, a dozen men of Swiss citizenry as the continued tradition dictated. All in attendance had been sworn to secrecy before the Pope and God, under threat of excommunication and death. I have it on good authority that the Swiss Guard has the skillset and blessing of the church to make good on such threats of violence.

The Pope stood on a raised dais, hands resting on the pages of a worn tome, bound in grisly looking leather, its pages containing the darkest magic. The Latin incantations he spoke were like a foul smoke, filling the chamber with a sense of dread. I could smell the fear on those around me. I could hear and see the constant shifting of men from one foot to the other with growing anticipation. Twelve other priests stood below him on the ground in a line, a grotesque reframing of the last supper, chanting the same words in a haunting monotone echo. Six other men, all thick-framed and muscular, now stood at the portal levers while Brother's Psalm, Job, Amos, Hosea, Micah, and Ezra stood in a line before the circular gate on the floor. Our party was dressed for an expedition, wearing short sleeve white cotton shirts, khakis with cargo pockets, and some Columbia hiking shoes. We were allowed a watch and a small black backpack containing two bottles of water, two protein bars, and a small emergency trauma kit. Brother Psalm's pack also included items for the exorcism he would perform. Leviticus stood behind the others; her eyes closed, holding a purple hairbrush with both hands pressed against her chest. From behind her, I leaned slightly to the right and saw loose strands of burgundy hair tangled in the barbs of the brush. It was the psychic item that would lead us to Jillian Vickers. It would help Leviticus create the psychic image inside her mind, using it as a compass to lead them to their target. It reminded me of a Bloodhound using a scent to track a fugitive.

I felt a prickling of dread in the back of my skull as the Pope went silent and the book he carried closed with a heavy thud. As the six sections of stone parted once more, a hiss of pressure was released, and the entire chamber was filled with the choking stench of sulfur and decay. A younger cardinal retched several times before he was able to stifle the sound with a hand clasped firmly around his mouth, but I didn't blame him. In truth, I also fought down a bit of bile that had come calling up my throat as the noxious smell entered my nostrils. As the stones sank into their recesses and the temperature inside the underground cathedral began to rise rapidly, the other priests around us brandished crosses and vials of holy water.

"I will pray for your safe return," the Pope said solemnly, drawing the cross in the air before us.

Brother Psalm nodded, then led us down the smoldering staircase into Hell. The stairs went straight down, inside what might have been a lava tube with tight walls and a low ceiling. I felt like I was inside the throat of a giant beast, heading toward its fiery belly. There was a grinding and scraping of sliding stones above us as the Hell Gate closed with a chilling finality. In that moment, I had never felt more cut off from the grace of God. Our group continued down the steps for close to an hour. Towards the bottom, the steps became chipped and fractured, eventually coming to a landing of black stone. We exited the tube onto a rocky plateau, comprised of sheets of slate, fractured and split to reveal deadly crevasses. Behind us was a sheer cliff face of reddish stone, rising into a hazy black sky. A half-mile ahead, I saw a structure far larger than anything I had ever thought possible. In many ways, it was like a giant cathedral but enforced with castle ramparts. There were tall pillars with sealed archways, reminiscent of Renaissance architecture, like Saint Peter's Bascilia or the Marciana Library. Brother Psalm stopped for a moment, letting Shaw, Kent, and myself take in the obscenely enormous building. Gashes in the surrounding landscape excreted liquid magma, bathing the structure in a crimson haze.

"Brother Psalm, what is this place?" I asked, keeping my voice low.

"It's called the Pandemonium," he said. "The first level of Hell."

"It means a place for all demons," Brother Amos added.

"There's a painting just like this at the Louvre!" Shaw exclaimed.

"Yes," Brother Amos said. "John Martin painted the Pandemonium one hundred and eighty years ago."

"He was here?" I asked. "He was in the Hell Retrieval Division?"

"No, but his brother Johnathan was for a time," Brother Amos said. "Back then, they simply referred to themselves as Hell Walkers. For a time, they tried to free as many souls as they could, but that brought on certain...attention from the demons in this place. Johnathan had an encounter in this place, and two of the men in his group died painful deaths. He returned in a state of madness, but it was discovered much later that he shared details with his brother."

"Quiet now," Brother Psalm called over the steady rumble from the fissures all around us.

The Pandemonium was so vast and obscured by darkness I couldn't tell where either end of the megastructure stopped. Shadows seemed to enshroud the building with an amalgam of dark swirling shapes, like black clouds or mist, that kept everything in a perpetual state of midnight. I couldn't tell if we were inside a vast cavern or standing on the surface of a rocky wasteland with an open sky above us. We carefully picked our way across the rocks until a long thin bridge came into view, a walkway carved from the same rock beneath our feet, leading to an oversized wooden door set into the outer wall of the Pandemonium. The door was inlaid with golden hinges, golden nails, and gilded symbols carved into the frame surrounding it. As we neared the bridge, I noticed gold worked into many aspects of the structures. Columns, pediments, arches, and domes all gave off a slight golden shimmer from the glow of burning magma or the firelight from torches lining the tops of the walls. I wondered who had lit all those torches as Brother Psalm stepped out first onto the crossing, a precarious strip of rock that gave a silent warning to take heed. To the left and right of the bridge were deep fissures in the rock, gashes like wounds carved from a giant blade. Far below, bright lava flowed like a river pouring out from the sun, promising a painful yet quick death.

I feared a sudden gust of wind could pull the entire party off the stairs to their death, going as far as to mention that notion to Brother Ezra.

"A cool breeze would be a pleasure, and you'll find none of those here," he said.

I wanted to inquire about the chances of a hot breeze, but he seemed resolved to stay silent, so I let the matter go and pressed on.

Levi was fidgeting with the straps on her backpack, pressing a hand to one of the side pockets on occasion. I knew how she felt, but I had something to prove to the other priests, so I pretended I wasn't on the verge of soiling myself at any minute. Once everyone in our party had crossed, the door behind me closed with a resounding thud.

To imagine the scale of the Pandemonium, it's necessary to take any normal proportions or dimension and multiply them a hundred-fold, if not more. We stood inside a foyer the size of an entire football stadium. The left and right wings of the building stretched off to both sides, spanning a distance in which I could not clearly discern the end. A hundred thousand burning candles lit oversized hallways lined with a dozen levels of steel doors, eliciting both a prison and a hotel. Ahead of us was a giant staircase, a hundred feet wide, large enough to hold an army. It descended into the lower levels of Hell, and I found myself looking to Levi in hopes Jillian was somewhere very close by. Levi must have read my face because she shook her head quickly from side to side, then clutched the hairbrush tight against her breast. A scattering of figures moved about shadows of the grand hallway, keeping their distance as they shuffled slowly along indiscernible pathways. The floor was covered in highly polished marble, inlaid with lines and ribbons of gold. The ceilings were vaulted high above our heads, ten stories at least. At first glance, we were standing in a palace of pure opulence. It was quiet to the point it chilled me, save for a soft scraping that echoed around the chamber like white noise.

"Not what you expected?" Brother Psalm's voice called from the head of the group.

The other priests parted, allowing him to take several steps closer.

"Look closer," Brother Psalm said. "There are plenty of horrors to be seen. Even on this level."

We walked towards the stairs, and as we did, I noticed deep cuts and scrapes carved into the polished floors. The mysterious figures came closer, and I was shocked to see what had once been a man hauling a large rock affixed to a chain shackled around his leg. He moved like a tripod, planting his knuckles onto the hard floor, then using his free leg to push while his chained leg stretched and dragged the heavy rock several inches forward at a time.

"Chain-draggers," Brother Amos whispered. "The longer they are down here, the worse they get."

To drive his point home, I saw a woman dragging a large stone by what looked to be a tail. Upon closer inspection, I realized her leg had become extremely deformed and elongated into the grotesque appendage. She projected almost no facial expression except the emptiness reflected in her pitiful stare. It was a look devoid of hope. She had accepted her fate, doomed to drag her burdens behind her until eternity ceased to be.

The floors beyond the foyer bore deep scars and lacerations, defaced and marred by the weighted stones to ruin any beauty that may have once been long ago. The walls, floor, and even ceiling had fissures and cracks running through them like the branching arms of a river. Bulging eyes stared back at me through the cracks, a few probing fingers, sometimes an arm or wrist. There were thousands, maybe hundreds of thousands of bodies wedged between the splits in the stone, trapped inside impossibly tight spaces in a crushing claustrophobic embrace. The hopelessness turned my stomach as I desperately tried to rationalize and compartmentalize the images of endless torture.

Levi opened her bag and removed a worn-out Carolina Tarheels ball cap, pulling the rim down low towards the bridge of her nose. She moved to the head of the line in front of Brother Psalm and led the party onto the staircase. Even the steps contained imprisoned souls that stared up, desperate and jealous, as we did our best to avoid stepping directly on the cracks.

The second floor was just as cavernous as the first, but the air was hotter, the feeling of anxiety growing stronger. There were more hallways containing hundreds of doors, some made of heavy wood, others metal at different oxidation stages. I heard screaming behind many of those doors, some from pain, others from anger, but they all held a note of suffering. I was greatly disturbed to find viewing slots on all the doors, fearing the implications that someone or something would be coming by soon to check on their occupants. Our group stopped so Levi could get her bearings, and Shaw and Kent ran into me, causing me to stumble. I turned back to chastise Shaw, but I saw his face was pale and drained of color. Kent seemed in worse shape, his left eye betraying a slight twitch when he tried to offer a fake smile.

"This place is cursed," whispered Shaw. "We shouldn't be here."

"Of course, we shouldn't be here!" I hissed. "But this is the job, and we will see it through."

"I..." Shaw trailed off, looking down.

I was standing on someone's outstretched fingers within the floor. I took a careful sidestep to my left.

"Have faith," Brother Amos said, reading the distress on Shaw's face. "The Lord will protect his faithful."

"Right," Shaw said, drained of all conviction.

Brother Amos nodded as if satisfied by his response, rejoining the other priests as they gathered around Levi.

She held the purple brush out in her right hand and raised her left, fingers spread wide as she scanned the area like a human antenna.

I felt myself drifting towards the nearest door, not meaning to, but not stopping myself either. I looked inside. I saw a man, his head held underwater in a stone basin by a cloaked figure. The man's arms thrashed wildly as his tormentor held him down until his body went limp. Moments later, the drowned man was revived, drawing himself up to take a breath of air. Before he could break the surface of the water, he was pushed back down to begin his frightening death, over and over. In Hell, there is no quick death, for if it came quickly, it simply has more opportunities to happen again and again.

"She's close," Levi said, eyes closed. "A little further ahead. On the left, I think."

"A little further ahead" turned out to be thirty more minutes of walking down the same hallway full of cries for help that would never come. We finally arrived at a steel door on the left side of the hallway, rashes of rust and flaking paint traveling up the side and near the hinges.

"She's in there," Levi said, handing the hairbrush to Brother Psalm.

She ambled to the back of the group and placed her hands on her head as she turned away. I felt the sudden urge to comfort her, but my thoughts were interrupted as Psalm cleared his throat, drawing my attention.

"She'll be fine," he said. "Let's go."

The door was barred from the outside, making a sharp creak as Brother Psalm pulled back the heavy deadbolt. Shaw, Kent, and I were ushered to the front of the line behind Brother Psalm as he opened the cell door. Jillian Vickers was sitting in a plain wooden chair in her underwear, arms and feet bound in rope, screaming at the top of her lungs. At first, she simply appeared mad, but after a moment, I noticed the floor and walls seemed to be moving. Thousands of tiny spiders poured out through openings in the stone and cracked marble. They moved like a single organism, covering her legs and thighs as she bucked against her restraints in vain. They were biting her as they went, skittering up her stomach and chest, her eyes wide with chaotic, primal fear. The spiders were on her neck, in her hair, and moving across her face as her screams reached a crescendo, forcing their way into her ears, mouth, and nose. She shook in her restraints, choking and convulsing as the spiders filled her throat. I was frozen in shock and repulsion. I hadn't noticed Brother Psalm digging in his bag, pulling out an ornate cross, and thrusting it in her direction. The cross had a faint glow, like a streetlamp, and its opaque rays beamed across Jillian's body. Where the dull light touched, the spiders evaporated like a smokey illusion. Brothers Hosea and Micah pressed past me, their silver crosses presented, followed by Brothers Amos and Job. The light had become blinding, and Jillian sat transfixed, like a deer in headlights. Her chest was heaving with rapid breathing, but I could tell that her torture had been put into a temporary limbo. Brother Ezra pushed past me, holding a small camcorder.

"Jillian," Brother Ezra called in a firm, clear voice. "Jillian Vickers. Can you hear me?"

Jillian was stunned, her eyes darting from side to side, like she had just been shaken from a deep sleep and her consciousness was still in a partial free fall.

"Jillian Vickers," Brother Ezra repeated. "Are you Jillian Vickers?"

"Yes," she whimpered. "I want to go home!" her lower lip curled and trembled. "Daddy, I'm sorry. It was an accident. Can I please come home?"

Brother Ezra thrust a photograph before her.

"Jillian, who is this woman? I need to know Jillian, please!" He demanded.

"My Aunt Cindy. Can I please go?" she pleaded.

"Almost Jillian. Who is this man?" he asked, producing another photograph.

"Papa. Papa Bill," she said. "Where am I? Where's my daughter?"

"You can see her soon," he said. "What music group did you see twice in concert?"

"Uh, um.."Jillian's eyes glazed over, and she swayed dangerously in her chair.

"Jillian!" Brother Ezra bellowed. "What music group?"

"R..radio...head," she answered.

"Very good, Jillian," Brother Ezra said, his voice softening. "One last question, and you can go home. Do you accept the love of Christ into your heart, denounce all sinful acts, and pledge your eternal soul to his holy name?"

"Yes!" Jillian cried out, bursting into tears. "God help me!" she wept.

Brother Ezra stepped back as Brother Psalm squared off before her, holding his cross out in one hand. The other held a vial of holy water that he flicked onto Jillian as he chanted out the deprecative formulas, prayers of exorcism, in practiced Latin. I watched the other priests chanting similar prayers, gripping their crosses, and felt an energy building in the room. Jillian must have felt it also because she stopped her rocking and sat upright, gripping the armrests tightly and turning her face to the ceiling. Her breath came in short bursts, her chest bouncing with each effort. I might have thought it was a seizure, but her face was calm, even hopeful. She cried unabashedly as tears flowed down her cheeks. The room took on a bright haze which I thought came from the crosses, but I soon realized it was Jillian. An aura of white light emanated from her body, spreading across her skin until she was a silhouette of radiant energy. Brother Psalm was shouting words, but I couldn't hear a thing, as if I was caught inside a vacuum. A sharp crack left a ringing in my ears, and Jillian was gone. Excited, I turned to Shaw and Kent, who both stood wide-eyed and open-mouthed.

"That was..." Kent began.

"A miracle," Shaw finished.

Brother Psalm looked at me, and though his whole presence spoke of exhaustion, he smiled.

"Hell lost another one," he said proudly.

I smiled back, grateful he had been my mentor during the trials. For Brother Psalm, it wasn't about the money, at least not entirely. I looked at the other priests and felt a sudden kinship with those six men. What I witnessed was incredible. I would join the Hell Retrieval Division. One day, I might even lead them as Brother Psalm did. I looked for Leviticus, but she wasn't in the room with the others.

"Brother Psalm," I said. "Where's Leviticus?"

The room went silent and tense as a bowstring. The men spilled out into the hall, and I followed.

"She's gone!" Brother Amos said, looking up and down the halls.

Brother Amos stared back into the room, taking a moment to think. I could see his mind revisiting memories, processing possibilities, and anticipating outcomes. Nobody spoke for fear of breaking his concentration. He looked up, and I saw understanding.

"It was the hat," he said. "We missed it. Leviticus had worn it all those other times. I thought it brought her comfort. She's been searching for someone!"

"Her psychic connection," I said. "Like the brush."

"Exactly," he said, his face lined with worry. "Everyone, it's time to go... now!"

"What does this mean?" I asked as everyone shoved their things into their bags and formed up in the hallway.

Brother Psalm motioned with his head for me to join him at the front of the line and we set off at a quick pace, just shy of a jog.

"She can't perform the exorcism, so she'll try to take them through the Hell Gate," Brother Psalm said, looking back down the stairs leading to lower levels.

"What happens if she does that?" I asked.

"A physical presence from Hell cannot cross back into the world of the living," he said. "It creates a paradox of the living dead, who only desire to kill and consume human life. If we are lucky, we will beat her to the gate and the Pope will close the portal, keeping the spirit trapped in Hell. Another possibility is that the Pope's guard will kill her as soon as she emerges."

"Any other possibilities?" I asked as we headed up the staircase, back towards the first floor.

"If the person Levi takes through the gate can manage to get past the guards and into the upper levels where tourists are allowed below the Vatican, it could spell disaster," Brother Psalm replied. "There could be an outbreak of death and destruction the world hasn't seen for centuries."

I thought about the frightening possibilities as we hurried up the stairs. It was hard to look ahead, feeling dwarfed by the scale of everything. I was like an insect in the presence of all the terrible splendor around me. Looking down was just as bad, if not worse. Eyes stared back, frantically searching, fingers groped, and moans of pain and loneliness floated up through cracks in the marble. I kept my eyes squinted, forcing my vision to remain slightly blurred by my eyelashes. We fell into a steady rhythm, making good time up the stairs and back to the massive foyer. I was vaguely aware that the Stone-draggers had stopped moving and stood as tall as their malformed bodies would allow, watching our party as Brother Psalm pushed open the large golden door and led us back onto the stone bridge.

We skittered across the bleak landscape, and I welcomed the hot black rock and stink of sulfur over the hopeless terrors inside the Pandemonium.

"Look," Brother Psalm shouted as he pointed towards the tunnel entrance set into the base of the cliff, still a couple of hundred yards away.

Two white shapes blinked out at the landing.

"Hurry!" Brother Psalm yelled, picking up the pace.

We were a hundred yards out, and my lungs were burning. A sharp cramp was announcing itself on my left side, and I did my best to silence it. I took slow, deep breaths, pressing my fingers into my abdomen. I tried to distract myself from the pain by imagining Levi, or whoever she really was, emerging through the gate into the Vatican, greeted by a hailstorm of bullets. I tried not to think of the alternative scenario, the one in which she unleashed a monster on the innocent families inside the city. My thoughts were interrupted when the ground lurched violently to the side, and we were all taken off our feet or sent stumbling.

There was a grinding vibration beneath my hands and feet as if some slumbering beast deep underground had awakened from its slumber and was clawing towards the surface. Ahead, the face of the cliff surrounding the tunnel entrance became blurry, and it took me several moments to realize the entire cliff was also shaking. Large chunks of rock started to break away and tumble through the air, smashing onto the flat ground below. As each slab of rock fell, a shiny golden reflection was revealed beneath. Piece after piece, a golden statue beneath was excavated. I was still on my knees, stunned like the others, as the entire image was finally revealed. A towering golden angel, wings spread, held a trumpet to its lips. The trumpet itself had been the rocky tube we had descended upon our arrival. Seeing the exposed angel in all its horrific glory, I knew that the gateway between our worlds had been constructed in Hell. The ground stopped heaving, and the mountains became still. A sudden hush fell over the land of the damned.

"Brother Psalm," Brother Amos called out, picking himself up slowly, the back of his shirt soaked in sweat. "What does this mean?"

A long and sustained blast of air emanated from the trumpet, billowing out sand like a blast of hot breath in the winter. The sound it made was a deep, rich note that was both painful and pleasant at the same time. Brother Psalm looked over our uncertain group, the muscles in his jaw tensing.

"Run," he commanded.

Although the pain in my side had redoubled, and I felt sure my heart would rupture, there was a certain exhilaration in running for my life. My bookbag had slipped one shoulder, but I let it fall away. We closed the distance quickly, fifty yards turning to thirty, then twenty. The entire team came to a sliding, fumbling halt as a figure stepped from the tunnel. He was tall and handsome, dark-haired and blue-eyed. His cheeks and chin were covered in short black stubble. He wore a fitted two-piece white suit covered in streaks and spatters of bright red blood. He looked pleasantly surprised to see us huddled together on the ground and took several more casual steps in our direction.

A *thump, thump, thump* came from the tunnel, and a second figure emerged, dragging the mutilated body of Leviticus behind him by one of her arms. It was a young man with short sandy-brown hair, fair-skinned and emaciated. I could see hints of facial features from Leviticus in his lined face, *a brother maybe*. An unsightly gash ran from the center of his left forearm to his wrist. *A suicide*, I thought.

Brother Ezra threw his hands up. "God, save your servants!" he shouted. "Protect us from this evil! Smite this Devil!"

The man in the white suit closed his eyes and raised his hands, mocking Brother Ezra, miming a whispered praise for the Lord and shaking his head slowly from side to side. Brother Ezra stopped praying and stared in disbelief. The handsome man squatted down and looked Brother Ezra in the eyes.

"God doesn't come down here," he said, spreading his hands out, then rising back to his feet. "And I'm not just any devil."

"Lucifer," Brother Psalm said like the words were broken glass in his mouth.

"That's right," Lucifer winked. "Your little group has been stealing from me for a long time. You're going to pay me back… with interest."

Brother Job, who had said no more than three words to me during my training, pulled out an old Ruger pistol from his backpack and shot Kent through his left temple. The blast was deafening, and I jerked away in surprise, throwing up my hands in a pointless self-defense. Brother Job turned and shot Shaw between the eyes, then shifted his wild stare onto me. The pistol was only a few feet from my face, wriggly back and forth in Brother Job's trembling hand. I could tell he desperately wanted to pull the trigger, to put a bullet in my head, but he couldn't.

I hadn't seen Lucifer's robed acolytes rushing towards us from the Pandemonium. The trumpet blast must have let them know their master had returned. Two of them clutched Brother Job, pulling his arm down towards the rocky ground.

"Thou. Shalt. Not. Kill," Lucifer said, approaching Brother Job and leaning down. "His rules, not mine," he smiled, pointing to the sky. Lucifer gently lifted the Ruger from Brother Job's hands and hefted it lovingly in his palm. "Such a beautiful invention." He pointed the pistol in Brother Job's face. "That's two more you owe me," he grinned. "You almost saved a third," he said, waving the gun in my face. He turned back to Brother Job. "Very brave. Very noble. But you're a murderer now," he continued. "And I've got a room for you."

A dozen more faceless torturers from the Pandemonium had marched out to meet their master, their faces concealed in unnaturally dark shadows. The two figures holding Brother Job jerked him onto his back by his arms and started to drag him away, his heels scraping as he stared helplessly back at me and tried to mouth unheard words. Lucifer stopped, looking annoyed. He turned to Levi's brother, who was still standing with his sister's wrist grasped in his hand, staring down in silence.

"You too!" Lucifer snapped.

The man hung his head and trudged back, pulling Levi behind him like one of the Chain-draggers.

"I'm sorry," Lucifer said, turning back, his face full of charismatic cheer. "Good disciples are so hard to find."

It sickened me how he enjoyed every minute of our perilous gathering.

"You knew what the church was doing, but you let them. Why?" Brother Psalm asked.

I couldn't believe Brother Psalm could remain so calm, let alone ask questions of the Devil. I tried to think of questions, anything to keep the conversation going. We were facing an eternity of suffering, and I was in no rush to begin my sentence. Sadly, I could only think of how scared I was; how much I wanted to see my parents, and how much I wished I had never joined the God damned Hell Retrieval Division.

Lucifer smiled. "Questions?" he mused at Brother Psalm. "Aren't you going to beg for mercy?"

"I've seen your kingdom," Brother Psalm replied coldly.

"Mercy is in short supply."

"Fair," he replied, smirking, unspoken threats hanging in the air. "As long as you kept opening the gate, I was free to cross over. While you were wasting your time, saving the unworthy children of Godless parents, I was out there," he pointed to the sky. "I was spreading the good news. We don't need *him* anymore."

The other robed acolytes quickly spread out and took hold of us, lifting us to our feet. Their strength was incredible. I tried to look at their faces, but all that stared back was an empty, dark void. I felt intoxicated with fear as Lucifer walked up and down our line, sizing us up. Lucifer and his bloody white suit ended up in front of Brother Psalm with a carefree smile on his face. I watched in wide-eyed anticipation as Lucifer held up his pointer finger, the nail coming to a sharp point. He bared his teeth as he carved an upside-down cross into the skin between Brother Psalm's eyes. Lucifer then pressed his thumb over the wound like a catholic ash cross and whispered his own dark prayer. Brother Psalm cried out in pain and struggled, but only for a moment. He took a sharp breath as his pupils expanded, filling both eyes and turning them black. The upside-down cross glowed white hot, then faded to a dull orange and eventually cooled to reveal unmarked skin, as if the mark had become a part of him. The whites of his eyes returned as the look on his face became calm and docile. The hooded figures released him, and he rose to his feet, a man at peace.

"Brother Psalm?" I asked, trying to read his face.

"It's alright, son," he replied. "Don't try to resist."

Lucifer moved down the line, carving his cross into each member's head. Brother Hosea and Amos resisted to no effect, Brother Micah wept and called out to God, and Brother Ezra accepted the mark as Brother Psalm had suggested. When Lucifer got to me, my heart was pounding, and I felt my insides run cold.

I tried to do as Brother Psalm had instructed and Brother Ezra had demonstrated, though I still cried out as Lucifer's nail dug into my skin. As he spoke his prayer or curse, my head felt filled with a dark cloud of smoke, choking out my thoughts so that only his will would remain. I knew that I should listen to Lucifer's instructions and obey without question, but something inside me remained inaccessible to his influence. It's been said that taking large doses of psychedelic substances like LSD and magic mushrooms can alter the user's consciousness in profound and lasting ways. *The psychological trials*, I thought. *Had they been meant for more than simply overcoming fears? Had my brain chemistry been altered? Were we immune to his control?*

"You're mine now. All of you," Lucifer said smugly. "Return to the Vatican. Have the book waiting for me in three days when I open the gate."

Yes, Lord, the words pressed at my mind, so I said them out loud. We all did, and Lucifer was pleased. We turned and fell into a single file line, Brother Psalm leading us once more, and began the long climb up the tunnel of the fallen angel.

As we headed back to the surface, we all carried a little piece of Hell with us, but the further we walked, the smaller it became. God knew what we would do when the stone gateway opened, and we stepped back into the land of the living. In three days, Lucifer was coming. He wanted the Pope's book of incantations and expected us to retrieve it for him. We had three days to either do his bidding, run like Hell, or stay, stand our ground, and wage war against the Devil.

THE FINAL RESTING PLACE

W et leather boots squeaked against the cold marble floor inside St. Augustine Mausoleum. Anna Furlough could barely form a coherent thought inside her head before the rough hands of her attacker squeezed them out. Anna stared up into a set of crazed eyes full of a terrifying fury. Beads of water and sweat dripped from the man's messy hair that framed his contorted face. Spittle formed at his lips as he strained with exertion. The pressure behind her eyes was unbearable as she wrestled with his hands around her neck, trying to release his grasp.

Anna twisted her head from left to right, trying to break the hold and find a way to steal a breath while she looked for a means of escape. The mausoleum was immense, paid for by her family's estate many years ago. Her mother was laid to rest, not even six feet from her place on the floor. The statue of an angel within stood silent guard over the dead, weeping a single tear, trapped in stone for all time. The tiles of marble alternated between black and white like a chess board as if to say life and death were just part of a game, a game Anna found herself losing.

She felt her chest heaving, an involuntary spasm of muscles that signaled the man's work would soon be finished. She heard the cries of a child but could not tell if the sounds were real or just imagined.

Is that my baby? She wondered. Is that my Lauren? With that final thought, Anna's heart stopped, and her body went limp.

Her soul departed like the floating lanterns she had watched as a small girl, rising towards the heavens with a steady glow. Anna could feel a gentle force pulling her away, calling her home. Her spirit looked down and saw the man looming over her lifeless body, his white-knuckled hands still around her throat. A dark rage was born within her ethereal form, a thirst for revenge that ignored the urge to float away. The memories of her life seemed to have gone on to that other place because she no longer recognized the woman lying on the floor. She couldn't name the little girl in the corner of the crypt, her knees tucked beneath her as she cried with hands cupped around her eyes to block out the noise. The one thing that did remain was Anna's hatred for the man she saw. She still heard a distant call, but she could ignore it. She wasn't going anywhere until she made him suffer.

Edward Pierce backed away from the dead woman on the checkered floor. His hands shook from the adrenaline and fatigue of squeezing her throat so tightly. The young girl in the corner of the mausoleum watched him fearfully as he got to his feet.

"It's done," he said, wiping the hair from his face. "She's gone now."

The lamplight flickered along the walls, threatening to extinguish. A sudden chill crept across Edward's arms, settling on the back of his neck. A shiver ran through his body, followed by the uncanny feeling of being watched.

"Who's there?" he shouted into the shadows around the crypt. "Come out!" he commanded.

The child was crouched in the corner, glancing about with fearful dismay. Edward paused as he and the girl made eye contact. She might have been seven or eight years old, just like the others. She had several smudges of dirt and grease on her face. Her clothes were old and worn, a shade of brown that was typical in the poorer districts.

Too poor for proper window locks, he thought. That's what made it so easy to grab them at night. Edward took a clumsy step forward and then stopped, waiting to see if the little girl would run, but she stayed frozen in place. Her eyes darted between him and the corpse on the floor, no doubt wondering if she would be next.

Anna's essence followed the man as he fled the mausoleum with the little girl in his arms. Her anger was acute, driving her after him into a moonless night. She glided along the ground as the leaves scattered in her wake, moving silently through the surrounding graveyard. Thoughts and memories flashed inside her awareness like strikes of lightning. She heard the echoing sounds of children laughing, which soon became shrill crying. The children. The missing children. Many had been taken, though remembering their names and faces was impossible. She was driven by feeling and intuition, stuck between the realms of the living and the lost.

Those same feelings talked to new possibilities within her. Anna focused her awareness as she closed in behind the man. The wind whipped and howled as she reached for him. Her hand disappeared into his ribs, and he cried out, tumbling down the small embankment leading to the iron gates of the graveyard. The little girl spilled from his arms, rolling along with him. She cried as she came to a stop near a pile of wet leaves, but at least she was still breathing. Anna turned to the man, watching him grip his side, still feeling the effects where her ghostly hand had passed through his flesh.

The calling for her soul was urgently pulling at her to leave the world of the living, but she wasn't ready. She had found a way to save her daughter and send the killer's soul to hell. The man scrambled on knees and elbows, reaching towards the girl, towards her Lauren. Anna burst forward, snatching at the man's leg. Again, her hand passed through his clothing, gripping at meat and bone. He howled in pain, sounding like sweet music in her mind. The man limped to Lauren, a resilient beast, scooping her back into his arms. He spun to face her, clutching her Lauren against his chest.

"You can't have her!" he cried out. "May hell take you!"

"Give me the girl!" she screamed, the grating sound of her voice like screeching echoes down a hallway. "Give me my daughter!"

"She's not your daughter!" the man yelled as he stood. "Don't you know who you are?"

Anna stopped, watching Lauren cling to the man. She wasn't afraid of him; she was afraid of her.

A blind rage filled Anna's awareness. She flew forward, plunging a hand into the man's chest. His eyes went wide, and he dropped Lauren. Anna's fingers snaked around his heart, and she started to squeeze.

There was an explosion of pain in Edward's chest as the ghostly hand moved through his coat. He dropped the girl, unable to breathe, let alone hold a child. He batted awkwardly at the arm of the spirit with clutched hands, but his fists moved through her like columns of smoke.

"Can't...have her," Edward struggled. "Not...yours." Edward's vision swam, and his daughter's face flashed before his eyes. "Damn, you...Mother Midnight!" The pain stopped suddenly as the spirit drew back. "You're...Mother Midnight," he gasped, "...taking children...while they...sleep. You took my Julie from me! I couldn't save her, but I found you!" The child had crawled back to him, her little arms wrapping around his neck. "I found you," Edward continued, "and I put an end to you in the crypt before you could kill again."

A piercing shriek emanated from the ghostly form as it writhed and contorted like a snake with its head removed. The girl buried her face in the back of his neck, but Edward had found his bravery to face her translucent form. He had already lost everything the night Mother Midnight had taken Julie. The police had been fruitless in their investigations. Perhaps if the children of the wealthy had gone missing, they might have committed more resources to the search. Edward had spent months piecing together the clues of the heinous crimes. Slowly, he had formed a picture of her habits, tracing the places she chose for her hunting grounds. Born to a prominent family, Anna Furlough's wealth and connections had helped her avoid detection and capture, allowing her free reign for almost two years. The money had finally led him to the Saint Augustine cemetery, where his wife and child were buried. The giant mausoleum in the center of the graveyard had served as the Furlough family crypt and Anna's secret killing room. It was only fitting that it became the very place of her demise.

◆●◆

As terrible memories flooded her consciousness, Anna screamed as the man spoke the name "Mother Midnight". Her monstrous deeds became apparent. The little girl, not her Lauren, had almost been her sixteenth victim. What evil had driven her all that time? She had tried to resurrect her Lauren with each child she took, dressing the girls in her beautiful summer dresses, giving them her toys, and promising to love them. In the end, they had never lived up to the daughter she lost.

The voice that had been calling Anna home now sounded threatening in her mind. She was not meant for fields of golden grain, shepherding her to eternal bliss with her ancestors. The voice was calling her to pay for her crimes. The man before her was no villain. He had been the justice sent to end her murderous obsessions. She had deserved what she had gotten in the crypt. The man deserved forgiveness, not damnation. Finally, in death, all had become clear to her. Anna moved toward the voice, choosing to face her judgment as the light of her essence faded into darkness.

Edward shuffled slowly back up the graveyard hillside, heading towards a plot of land he knew all too well. He slumped to the ground near a pair of matching gravestones engraved with the names of his beloved Vivian and his little sunshine, Julie. He pressed his fingers into the damp soil, praying he could hold them again, but knowing only empty shells remained below the dirt.

"Forgive me, love," Edward said with tears in his eyes. "I took a life to save others, but I've still become a murderer. I pray that God will forgive me and grant me passage through the gates of heaven."

The rescued child surprised Edward as she took his face in her little hands. She smiled upon him with eyes that held wisdom and knowledge beyond her years. She gave a subtle nod as if answering his internal prayers. Edward felt a weight lift from his soul and freely offered tears of joy.

Overtaken with exhaustion, he laid his head down on the patchy grass and closed his eyes. The world grew lighter as dawn prepared to brighten the sky with the sunlight of a new day. The little girl, now safe from harm, nestled against his side, burrowing beneath the flap of his brown coat for warmth. The sun finally peaked above the horizon, and the light kissed his face as Edward drifted off into a deep sleep.

MISSING PERSON

Howard Allen crossed the wood panel floor of his living room towards the kitchen. He passed a wall calendar turned to October. The twelfth day had been circled with the words 'Big Thirty' drawn in red marker. He rubbed his stomach, checking to see if his body had already started to betray the march of time. He still felt a few ab muscles safely tucked under a thin layer of cushion and counted himself better off than most. He scratched at some fresh stubble on his jawline and remembered he was craving a cup of hot coffee. Halfway to the kitchen, one of the boards made a pronounced creak, like stepping on a sore joint. He stopped in place and rocked from heel to toe, trying to locate the source and replicate the sound without success. He gave up and finished the ten remaining paces to reach his coffee maker. The entire downstairs was humble in size, larger than a single-bedroom apartment, but not by much. He had chosen to sacrifice space to avoid noisy neighbors like the ones that had plagued him during his college years. Howard had always preferred quiet solace to the obnoxious partying that was considered a staple in the college experience. Living alone didn't require much space anyway, and he found comfort in the solitude. He had been done with schooling for several years, earning a bachelor's degree in human studies, which had not yet been put to good use. He currently worked manual labor jobs, which gave him a sense of satisfaction and brought in more money than the jobs available in his degree of study. He had once considered applying for a career in human resource development but eventually decided that the resulting desk job would be like a slow death.

His father, Thomas Allen, had been an intelligence officer in the United States Army. The man had been stern with him growing up, leaning heavily on basic training-style parenting to keep his behavior in line. Over the years, his father had softened, partially due to old age but also from things he had seen and done during his military career. As a teenager, Howard had understood very little of war or the effects it could have on the psyche. Later in life, when Thomas stopped talking, his mother attributed his father's behavior to post-traumatic stress disorder, but the way his father acted never aligned with what Howard would describe as combat stress. In fact, during the early years of Thomas's career, he had been eager to share stories of strange lands, heroism, and comradery during his combat deployments. One such story occurred during an extended deployment to Saudi Arabia during the Gulf War. He talked at lengths of remote villages and giant mountains with underground tunnels that could stretch on for what felt like miles. During a classified research operation, their travels brought them to vast lava fields in the region of Harrat Rahat, a name Howard had enjoyed repeating. There had been hundreds of ancient stone gates littering the area, placed by an ancient people that were no longer alive to tell the story behind their unique creation. Some of the gates were even covered in hardened lava, adding more intrigue to why anyone would build monuments in such an inhospitable location. The soldiers took to calling the area the Gates of Hell, which he had found fitting. One particular gate seemed larger than many of the other several hundred they had identified. Upon closer inspection, they had discovered a sealed entrance that they opened using military-issue blasting cord. Once inside, chiseled lava rock steps descended into vast open lava tubes and caverns. The further down into the cave his team went, they developed a type of brain fog and became easily disoriented. During his story, he drifted off into a sea of thought for several moments until he remembered *the box*, which snapped him back to reality. He ran out of the living room, straight back to the master bedroom to retrieve a small wooden box no bigger than a shoebox. It was within this box he kept his most treasured artifacts.

Howard filled his coffee maker with water from the kitchen sink and set it to brew. It came to life with an orchestra of bubbles and hisses. He thought about the old wooden box that once belonged to his father, which now belonged to him, nestled safely under his bed. Six figurines that were more like tiny totems, no larger than a can of Coke, rested inside the box in circular slots lined with a soft felt-like material. The figures themselves were each carved from various materials. Some were identifiably wood, while others resembled a dark stone and even possibly bone. The figures were fantastical creatures, some having multiple arms and legs, even multiple heads. Several had twisted limbs, contorted in uncomfortable poses, often accompanied by looks of pain or anguish. His favorite totem was of a beautiful woman carved out of smooth, polished magma. Her hair was full of different-shaped eyeballs, but he liked to imagine them as jewels. One was a mixture of a man and a rat, or possibly a mole. Another had a beard covered in barnacles, like an old pirate captain who drowned at sea and eventually became a part of the ocean floor. The fifth had been sheared in half, leaving a set of legs that did not seem human. The last was a mosaic of open mouths and staring eyeballs. He dreamed of the figures sometimes, breaking free from their earthly containers, growing tall as giants, the world gathering at their feet.

Howard's thoughts of his father and the mystical keepsakes were disturbed by the sharp tone of his automatic coffee maker finishing its brewing cycle. He poured himself a steaming cup of black coffee and padded his way to the living room to slump into his worn leather recliner.

Halfway back, the familiar creak of a loose floorboard sang its distress, demanding his attention. Frowning, he squatted down, placing his cup on the floor beside him. He used his broad shoulders and muscular arms to press into the floorboards like he was giving CPR compressions. He pushed in a circular pattern, searching for the noise, but was unable to reproduce the irritating call.

"Damn it," he muttered to himself.

Howard stood up, resulting in an even louder croak from the wooden planks. He cursed out loud and dropped to his knees, frantically pressing at the floor, moving in a clockwise circle. He knocked over his coffee cup, looking back as a puddle of dark liquid spread out across the floor, steam rising like a foggy lake in the early morning hours. A loud knock at the front door drew his attention away.

A striking young woman in her mid-twenties was standing on the other side of the door when he answered. She had smooth, long blonde hair draped around soft, clear skin, except for a small patch of freckles across the bridge of her nose. Her beauty was slightly tempered by dark rings under her eyes, maybe caused by a lack of sleep, excessive crying, or both.

"I'm Alicia Hatfield," the woman began in a small wispy voice. "Have you seen this woman?" She held up a photo of a woman with a lighter hair shade and a pleasant smile, a backdrop of purple flowers behind her."

Howard stared at the photo, noting a resemblance to the woman, with the addition of her hair and dozens of age lines that adorned the corners of her mouth and eyes.

"I'm sorry, I haven't," he said, clearing his throat, unsure what to say next.

Alicia continued with what sounded like a rehearsed speech, probably recited many times already. She was searching the neighborhood, looking for her mother, Tabitha, who had gone missing the night prior. Alicia explained her mother was in the early stages of dementia, causing her mental state to deteriorate quickly. She was becoming confused easily, forgetting where she was or who she was with. She had also begun wandering off without warning and had recently been found two blocks away from their home by a concerned neighbor.

"I'm sorry," he said again when she finished, offering another empty apology, like most people do when they can offer little else in the face of tragedy.

As sleep deprived and upset as she appeared, there was still something magnetic in her eyes. While living alone had its benefits, so did getting to know an attractive young woman. He figured they could find her mother quickly, and afterward, she could allow him to take her out for a coffee to show her gratitude.

"Maybe I can help you look," he said, eyebrows raising, hoping he sounded friendly and not like a lonely man with ulterior motives.

Alicia looked down and frowned, lips pursed, as she stood quietly in his doorway. After what felt like an age, she met his eyes and gave a weak smile.

"I don't want to impose," she said, a hint of color on her cheeks.

"It's no problem," he quickly added. "I could use some air. Just let me grab my jacket."

Howard turned before she could protest and went for a lightweight jacket hanging on the far wall of the house. As he headed back to the doorway, his spilled coffee caught his attention. The pool of dark liquid had shrunken rapidly, receding between a previously unseen sliver between the floorboards. *The creak!* He thought triumphantly. He left his cup sitting in its place on the floor, determined to find the loose board and fix it once he returned.

Howard and Alicia left together, walking the streets, stopping by a dozen or more houses, asking the same questions, and showing the picture of her mother. They searched for hours, traveling miles on foot as the sun moved overhead in its pathway toward the horizon. During their time together, he learned that Alicia preferred to go by Alice, that her father had passed away six years prior from lung cancer, and that Alice was going to school to be a nurse so she could take better care of her mother during the later stages in her life. It didn't seem fair that someone so young and hopeful for the world had been dealt so much hardship and loss. He wanted more than ever to help her find her mother, to give her a reason to let him into her life. He pictured her smiling as they found Tabitha, holding her as she cried with relief. A woman like Alice could change his life. A woman like her could help make him a better man.

They continued their search, looking up and down streets, checking off houses block after block. As the sun finally began to set and the streetlights came on, Howard started to feel an acute pain building in the back of his head that continued to intensity despite his best efforts to ignore it. *Had he eaten today?* As they neared a street intersection six blocks from his house, a wave of nausea and vertigo struck him, forcing him to stop and steady himself on a nearby telephone pole.

"Howard, are you alright?" Alice asked.

He waved off Alice's concern but soon doubled over.

"Howard!" she cried out.

He cursed himself, coming up into a sitting position against the metal pole. The pain in his skull and his pride were competing for supremacy.

"I'm so sorry, Alice," he apologized, trying to assure her that he really wanted to keep helping. His head swam, his vision becoming spotty.

"Do you need a doctor?" she asked, patting her pockets like she was looking for her phone.

"I'm fine," he lied, squeezing his eyes shut, then opening them wide, trying to release even the slightest amount of pressure. "I...I just need to get home to rest."

Howard picked himself up, turned, and stumbled away, leaving Alice standing alone with a look somewhere between disappointment and concern. He knew how bad it looked, but he couldn't stop himself. He had to get home. The night took on a claustrophobic feel as he made his way down long stretches of road that seemed to lengthen in the shadows. He soon became lost and disoriented, desperate to find a landmark or beacon to guide him back home. Several times along the way, he was forced to stop, jamming his fingers into the base of his skull, dragging them across his temples to meet in the center of his forehead. He took his thumbs and gradually pressed them harder and harder into the top of his eye sockets. He increased pressure until the pain intensified to the point he felt sick, then he removed his fingers to let the pain back off, subsiding enough for him to continue walking for several more minutes. He made his way past darkened alleys he dared not look down. He felt his heart beating inside his head, a steady drumbeat that brought a new wave of dizziness, like his brain would swell and hemorrhage. His vision narrowed, and he felt the darkness like a physical presence enshrouding him, beckoning him down into a world beyond his own reality. He thought of the lava fields from his father's stories and their worn steps leading down beneath the earth. Something was waiting at the end of those ancient steps, calling his name.

Howard woke up the following morning in a daze, his head perched at the edge of his mattress, his arm hanging off the side of the bed like a pendulum. He blinked away the sleep from his eyes and sat up. A string of saliva stretched from his pillow to his face before snapping and clinging to the bedsheet. His mouth tasted sour as he dragged his tongue over his teeth.

"Oh God," he moaned, smoothing down a cow lick and stroking his cheeks, reminiscing without delight at his embarrassing display from the night before.

With an additional sting of self-pity, Howard realized that he hadn't even asked Alice for her number. He rose from bed with a groan, right knee popping, and headed to the kitchen. Judging by the light coming into the house, it was still early morning. His coffee cup still sat in its place on the floor, a small dark stain soaked into the surrounding wood. He may have screwed up his chances with Alice, but at least *that* was something he could fix.

He went to his junk drawer in the kitchen and found a long, flat-head screwdriver, a chip missing from the red plastic handle. He started some fresh coffee and got to work trying to pry up the wooden floor panel so he could re-seat it and be rid of the troublesome sound once and for all. As he knelt before the suspected board, he leaned in, scanning the details of the wood.

He was shocked to find a small indention on the side of one of the panels at the intersection where it joined with two others. His intrigue multiplied as the screwdriver fit perfectly into the tiny grove, like a key made for a specific lock. He pushed down on the screwdriver grip and heard a soft *thump* as the board was released from its snug hold. In the absence of light beneath, a new panel of black had taken the board's place, obscuring any view of the foundation below. The air drifting up smelled damp and earthy, making Howard wrinkle his nose.

He continued to remove boards with little resistance, widening the hole until he had pulled enough panels to squeeze his shoulders through and gain access beneath the floor. He grabbed a small flashlight from the kitchen and shined it into the opening, revealing a compacted patch of dirt about five feet below. It struck him as an excessive gap for a simple crawl space, more like an unfinished basement, but he couldn't be sure until he went down and saw for himself. He paused, one foot dangling into the darkness, the remaining floorboards seeming like jagged teeth inside a grisly mouth. *It's fine*, he told himself. *Nothing to be worried about.* He took a deep breath, silencing his mental opposition, and dropped down onto packed earth.

The crawl space was far more expansive than he had imagined, stretching beyond the borders of the house's foundation by at least double the size. The ceiling was still low enough that he had to crouch, duck-walking around as he scanned the ground with his flashlight. The air was hot and stuffy, tiny droplets of sweat already starting to leak from his forehead and lower back. He scanned the ground with his light, sweeping the beam in uniform rows like he was reading a book. The hard-packed dirt gave way to looser soil the further he moved away from the hole above, the light from his living room shining down behind him like a holy projection.

He stopped abruptly when he spotted a large tuft of wispy white strands protruding from the soil like a sprout of weeds. He felt an icy stab of fear in his gut, mixed with a sick curiosity. He crouched down close, letting the beam of light cut through the fine strands. *Please be an animal*, he prayed. *Please be mold, anything but*...the white fibers lit up as slices of light passed through them, and nausea boiled up inside his stomach...*human hair*. Alice had described her mother as having very similar hair to hers, and the ones he saw were indeed blonde strands. He scanned around the ground, noticing lines of disturbed earth, indicating a recent shifting of the soil.

"How?" he whispered to himself, feeling his hands shake but helpless to make the stop.

He felt locked in a nightmare; the air was suddenly thick in his throat, and he was unable to manage a full breath. The damp smell quickly turned foul, like a dead animal left on the side of the road to bake in the sun. The silence in the crawl space made his ears ring, making him feel isolated but not entirely alone. Dark thoughts flooded his mind. *If Tabitha was buried under his house, who had put her there? What would he say to the police? He would be blamed! He would be charged as a murderer and sent to prison! If he tried to move or get rid of the body, he would be guilty in his own right.* Howard needed time to think. He hurried to the opening but stopped at the threshold of light. *What if the killer was inside the house?* He imagined a figure standing above the hole, looking down on him with an axe held high, ready to split his head open as he emerged from the floor.

"Shit," he hissed, looking back towards Tabitha's grave, weighing the choice in company.

He shuddered, held a breath, and popped up through the hole in the floor, arms raised defensively. His paranoia was met with silence and the light of a clear day coming through the windows. He lifted himself up and hastily returned the wooden slats to their original position, rushing to the kitchen sink to clean himself off. He made the water hot to the verge of pain, scrubbing his fingernails furiously, cursing in hissed whispers.

Howard spent the rest of the morning pacing every square inch of his modest living space, trying to find a solution but always ending on the worst imagined scenario. *Nobody would believe him. It would be jail or the electric chair.*

"I need air," he told himself. "*You* need air."

As he turned to the door, there was a gentle rapping against the wood, making him jump and bite the side of his tongue. He opened cautiously, surprised to see Alice standing in his doorway for the second time. She looked more rested, the rings around her eyes less pronounced. He swallowed the taste of copper, chewing at the cut on his tongue, and tried to push out the thoughts of Tabitha buried underneath the floorboards. He desperately wanted to tell Alice, but how could he? All he could do was hurt her with the truth or lie and buy himself some time. He forced a weary smile onto his face.

"Alice, what are you doing here?" he asked, burying his hands inside his pants pockets to keep them from shaking.

"You took off the other night so quickly. I was worried about you," she said.

"Worried about me?" He blurted out.

"Of course. You spent so much of the day helping me; it's the least I could do," she said kindly.

Despite washing up, he felt dirtier than ever. With everything Alice was going through, she still had room to worry for others. He had the answer she was searching for but would keep it hidden for his own sake. His own safety. His own survival.

With an effort, he forced his lips into a smile. "I'm fine. It was just a migraine, and I'm so sorry I left you like that."

"Howard, it's fine. You're only human. I realized we never exchanged numbers, so I just thought I could stop by. I hope that's not too forward of me," she said, tucking the sides of her long hair behind her ears.

"Oh, please, don't ever think that!" he insisted, maybe too eagerly. "You are going through so much right now. Have you heard anything?"

"Nothing," she said, looking down. "I called the police department over and over, and they can't tell me anything!" Her shoulders sagged, and she cupped a hand across her eyes in a weak attempt to hide her tears.

Howard didn't know what else to do, but step towards Alice

and embrace her in a strong, comforting hug. His heart fluttered as she sank into his chest, her hair smelling like fresh rain and flowers.

"I know you're scared, Alice, but we're going to find her, I promise," he said, trying to be reassuring. Without thinking, he gently kissed the top of her head. She pulled away sharply, putting several feet of distance between them.

"Howard, what are you doing?" she asked with an air of offense in her words.

He was shocked by the repugnant look on her face.

"Alice, I..." he began, stalling to find the words to say.

"What do you think this is? I asked for help to find my mom, not start a relationship! I thought you wanted to help me?"

"I do; I'm sorry, I didn't mean...I'm sorry, I thought..."

"You thought what? That you would help me look for my mom, and I would sleep with you?"

"No, I just felt a connection. I was trying to comfort you. I don't want in your pants!" he pleaded.

Alice stopped yelling and took a deep breath. She let out a joyless laugh, trailed by more tears.

"I'm sorry, Howard. I shouldn't have yelled at you like that. I know you are trying to help. I'm the one that showed up and knocked on your door."

To his surprise, she moved past him and walked further into the house, wiping her cheeks dry. She crossed the living room towards the kitchen, pausing as the floorboards creaked and groaned beneath her feet, a sharp note cutting into the silence.

"Oh, that was loud," she said, looking back towards Howard, then froze when she saw his face.

He had been so focused on tracing her footsteps across the floor, trying to predict her path, that he had failed to maintain his mask of calm. He immediately relaxed the muscles in his face and straightened up, but he knew the damage had been done. A dark seed of curiosity and doubt had been planted inside her mind. He could already see it sprouting into the twisted revelation it would surely become.

"What is it?" she asked, looking down.

"It's nothing," he answered quickly. He could feel a cold ball of panic growing inside, spreading like poison. He needed to get her out of his house before his nerves dragged him into a full-on panic attack.

"No, it's something," she pressed. "You're very pale, Howard."

The more he wanted to end the conversation and get her away from the loose floorboards, the more she seemed to root herself in place, silently demanding answers he couldn't give. She rocked back and forth in place as if taunting him. The creak had become a shrill cry, piercing the awkward silence that permeated the room.

"It's nothing," he repeated. "I'm really sorry for my behavior earlier. Honestly, I'm still not feeling very well. I think I just need to lie down and get some rest. I'd be happy to help you keep looking later."

Alice stood planted several feet above her mother's dead body, scanning Howard with her eyes, looking for cracks in his foundation.

"Please, Alice, I really just want to lay down," he said, almost pleading. "I'm really sorry."

She looked down at the floor, and he imagined she could see all the way through, like she had x-ray vision, or the floor was made of glass. Finally, to his relief, she offered a constructed smile and moved back to the front door, stepping through the threshold.

"Goodbye, Howard," she said with a finality that sent shivers down his spine.

"Will I...see you again?" he asked.

"Of course," she said. "I'll see you soon."

He stood in place for an hour after she was gone, feeling sick, frozen by guilt and fear. There had been an edge to how Alice said "soon". The solution to his problem had been like a worm, slowly squirming towards his core. He knew he would have to move, to act. Alice was starting to suspect something was wrong; he had seen it on her face. He had his task, and the clock was ticking. He would have to move the body.

That night Howard removed the floorboards and stacked them uniformly against the far wall as ceremoniously as he could manage. He tossed down a waterproof tarp, shovel, and small spade into the hole, making a metallic clang as they hit the packed dirt. He worked his fingers inside rubber dish gloves and cut on his flashlight. He tried to ignore the feeling of being watched but still shone the dull beam into each corner, just to be sure. Slowly, carefully, he made his way to Tabitha's body, tracing her outline with the small spade. Several times, however, he misjudged the placement of her limbs underground, wincing as he felt the small metal tip of his spade drag against stiff human flesh. The more he disturbed the earth, the more he became aware of the stench of decay emanating like a volcanic fissure bubbling up from the ocean floor, filling the entire chamber with the smell of death.

After several inches of dirt had been shifted to the side of the body, it became clear that Tabitha was lying on her stomach, left hand pinned by her side and right arm bent like it was waving goodbye. Most of her blonde hair was matted against the back of her head, flattened, and caked with dirt. A scuffling sound in one of the corners spun Howard around, scanning the walls with a beam of light, only to reveal more bare earth. Once again, he had the haunting feeling of being watched. He fought against paranoia and his disgust, resuming to loosen the dirt around Tabitha's ribcage. By the glow of his flashlight, he could tell she had been wearing a pink cashmere sweater and leggings that had the appearance of jeans. She wasn't wearing shoes, which left her ensemble incomplete, making him feel even worse. *Even the dead deserve some dignity*, he thought.

An hour later, shirt stained with sweat and feeling light-headed, he was finally ready to roll Tabitha from her shallow grave. He fetched the tarp and spread it out in a large square beside her, the material crinkling loudly in the quiet chamber. *This is it*, he thought with dread. The idea of seeing her face made his knees weak and his guts churn. He crouched onto the tarp, leaned over her body, and grabbed her sweater near the shoulder and waist. He took several deep breaths, trying to build his resolve, and pulled, rolling her over. While he knew he could simply close his eyes, a perverse curiosity inside made his want to look, if only for a moment.

Howard screamed. He barely recognized the high-pitched shriek leaving his lips as his own. He cried out again and again, like an involuntary response he could no longer control until his voice went horse. The world spun around him, and he tasted bile at the back of his throat, making him cough and retch.

"Alice," he croaked, staring into her cold, dead eyes. "Alice!" he screamed.

Alice's skin was a blotchy blue-grey, her open eyes clouded with a hazy film. Tiny white larvae danced at the corners of her mouth and inside her nose. Howard collapsed to his knees and vomited onto the tarp. He pushed himself up and tried to dart away but slipped on the contents of his stomach, falling to his chest as the air left his lungs. He rolled onto his side, gasping for air.

"Why?" he managed, hugging his arms across his chest. He shut his eyes tight, gently rocking. "This isn't real," he tried to assure himself, desperate to believe. "It's not real," he repeated, pulling himself back from the point of hysteria. "It's not real!" he angrily shouted as if he could bully himself into accepting the words.

After a dozen more affirmations, he rose to a sitting position, shining his light back onto Alice's body.

"It's not..." Howard paused his mantra, noting the small patch of freckles dotting the bridge of Alice's nose. "Real," he breathed.

He tried to remember what Alice had been wearing earlier that day, what she had been wearing the first time they had met. The image of a pink cashmere sweater and jean leggings filled his mind, and he saw her like a figure from a lucid dream.

There was a sound of bare feet padding on earth, a shuffling in the darkness. He cut at shadows with his flashlight once more, but this time someone was staring back. It was like looking into a mirror that was also a gateway to hell. Howard saw his own face looking back, but it was a version of himself he could only imagine in a nightmare. His doppelganger was gaunt and dirty, naked and hunched over. He rested on his haunches, his hands flat on the ground like a primal beast, bloody fingertips picking at the dirt beneath him. His hair was longer, dark, and matted to his forehead. The *Other Howard* snarled with the right side of his mouth, displaying a row of rotting teeth. Other Howard dashed forward on hands and feet in a half-gallop. He was on top of Howard before he could even react. Howard was pinned down; Other Howard's dirty red fingers snaked around the side of his face and pushed his left cheek down into the loose soil.

"What are you?" he managed to blurt out.

"I'm you," Other Howard laughed with a coarse, scratchy voice, his breath smelling like death itself. "We are one."

"No!" Howard screamed, struggling to get up, but the Other Howard kept him pressed down with little effort.

"We've got to keep digging, you and I," Other Howard spoke softly, his hot breath choking Howard's nose. "She's down there, waiting for us."

"Who's waiting?" Howard sputtered into the dirt.

"Mother. You've seen her in your dreams. She's always close."

Other Howard's hand started to slip down around Howard's throat, squeezing harder and harder.

"Please...stop..." Howard pleaded.

Darkness closed in around Howard in a tunnel with his grotesque counterpart on the other end, an unhinged smile on his face. Howard felt himself slipping into a void, cold and alone.

Howard woke up gasping for air in the dark, batting his hands at empty black space. He sprang up, knocking his head beneath the low wooden ceiling that doubled as the living room floor. There was a flash of white behind his eyelids, followed by a searing pain in the top of his skull. He fell to the ground, coughing forcefully to move air back into empty lungs. The kitchen lights had been turned off, and no traces of morning sunlight had made their way into the pit below the house. He felt trapped, buried alive in his fear. He swept his hands around in a panic, searching for his flashlight, praying he didn't grab hold of Alice's corpse by mistake. He found the flashlight by his foot and snatched it up, holding it close to his chest as he switched it on.

Alice's body had vanished from the tarp, and the hole he had dug had been filled back in, the dirt packed down smoothly. The abusive aroma of mildew and rotting skin lingered in the air, foul traces serving as a reminder of the dead. He snapped to attention, remembering Other Howard, spinning in all directions like a frantic lighthouse, but Other Howard was gone.

Howard found his way back to the hole in the floor leading into his living room. He hoisted himself up, arms shaking, and rolled onto his back. Still lying supine, he shone his flashlight on a clock on the wall near the front door. The time read a quarter past three in the morning. *The witching hour.* He squeezed his eyes tightly shut, terrified he could no longer tell what was real anymore, and tried to listen out for sounds of Other Howard, but all was quiet. *Where had he gone? Why did they look alike? And what mother was he talking about?*

"God, help me," he whispered.

Did last night really happen, or was it all a twisted nightmare? The thought of ever going back beneath the floorboards made him feel sick. Howard crawled to the bathroom on his hands and knees, feeling too weak to stand, straining as he pulled himself into the bathtub. He turned on the shower, laying back as cold jets of water soaked his clothes, sending dark ribbons trailing towards the drain. He watched the circling water, barely registering the chill on his skin. Once the water grew hot enough to steam the room, he removed his shirt and pants, dropping them with a heavy plop on the tiled floor. He slumped back, feet outstretched, and lay still until the hot water ran out.

Howard eventually climbed out, shivering as he dried off, and threw on a fresh pair of clothes. He then returned the wooden planks to their place, restoring the living room floor and closing whatever portal he had conjured by removing them. He moved to the couch and sank into the cushions, exhausted and shaken. He longed for sleep but feared what dreams would come. His heavy eyelids blinked once, then twice, then it was morning. The abrupt change in time struck him like a slap, followed by the confusion that was becoming far too common. *Had he slept?* Harsh light spilled into the house as a steady thumping grew louder and louder in his ears. He peered over the back of the couch apprehensively, settling his eyes on the sealed entrance to beneath the house. A sudden knock at the door sent him flailing, spilling to the floor as he drew up his arms in a defensive response. He froze, heart pounding, and waited. Another loud knock followed.

"Howard, are you there?" a familiar voice called out. "It's Alice!"

Dead Alice. He told himself. *Decomposing Alice. Buried Alice.* There was a third knock, more forceful than the others.

"Howard?" Alice asked again.

"Is this real?" he called out to the door.

"What?" she asked. "Howard, is that you?"

"It's me!" he yelled, clamping a hand over his mouth, rebuking himself for speaking.

"Are you going to answer the door?" she asked with a hint of playfulness in her voice.

He pounded his temples with his palms as if it might sift out reality from make-believe. He rose slowly and walked to the door, his knees ready to buckle at any moment. He swung the door open, stepping back to create a buffer between him and the front porch. Alice stood smiling, wearing low-cut jean shorts, a white tank top, and white running shoes as clean as if they had just come out of the box. She had her hair in a ponytail and wore a light layer of makeup, just enough to accentuate her features but not overpower them. She was shifting from one foot to the other, almost beaming with happiness; her smile was like warm sunlight on his skin.

"Alice," he said, lost in her kind face. "What's going on? You look...happy."

"I am!" she blurted out. She rushed forward and embraced Howard for the second time. "They found my mom!

She's ok!"

A feeling of relief crashed into him like a wave, forcing him to hold the door with one hand and Alice with the other to stay upright.

"They found her two counties over, shopping at a local supermarket. She had no idea how she got there. I'm headed to see her now, and I was hoping you would come with me. I know she would love to meet you."

"Oh, my God, that's...that's great news," he said, trying to stay in the moment with Alice, allowing himself to feel the comfort of their bodies pressed close together.

This is real, he told himself. *This feels real*. He took his hand off the door and pretended to rub his eyes as he wiped away tears. Alice took his other hand and led him outside, her contagious smile spreading to the corners of his mouth as they descended the steps. Howard squinted against the sun, letting himself be led by one hand onto a pathway made of dirt.

"What?" he asked, smile slipping as he let go of Alice's hand and turned back towards his house.

Howard and Alice stood in a clearing in the woods, a small log cabin sitting where his house had just been, the roof slightly sagging under the weight of thick green moss. Tall grass and overgrown hedges butted up against the left side of the glorified shack, the right wall propped up by a large stack of rotting firewood. Several varieties of mushrooms had sprouted from the decomposing pile, spreading to the side of the cabin like a rash. He stepped back towards the derelict structure, unsure if he would see a rundown cabin or the home he knew inside. He froze, almost stumbling; the door was slightly ajar, a pair of eyes watching him from the shadows inside. Other Howard's face appeared in the slit of the open door, his expression something between a dare and an invitation. A gentle hand hooked Howard by the chin and spun him away.

"Come on, Howard, it's time to go," Alice said, a firmness to her voice that he found impossible to deny.

They walked together down a winding path that snaked through a dense forest. Alice made small talk, commenting on the beauty of the woods or her excitement for him to meet her mother, Tabitha. Howard felt stuck in a waking dream, sensing the world blur around him, losing large chunks of time, and finding himself at new points in the trail every time he blinked. He wanted to stop, to sit down and catch his breath, but Alice pulled him further onward. Finally, when he could take no more, Howard pulled back, snatching his hand away.

"Alice, stop. Please," he said, eyes shut tight to keep the scenery from changing again. "I just need a minute, please."

"Of course, Howard," she said, her voice full of the same good cheer they set off with. "But just so you know, we're here!"

Howard opened his eyes and gasped, staring at a monumental estate, a mix between a castle and a mansion.

"Wait!" he said, eyes widening. "I know this place. This is the Biltmore House!"

Howard had spent his youth near the mountains of North Carolina, visiting family in the city of Asheville, driving up and down the Blue Ridge Parkway as he took in the scenic view. The Biltmore House had been a go-to tourist spot during Christmas time, the halls lit with hundreds of individually decorated trees. Howard felt sick again, thinking of his home in Hollowell, Maine, where he was born and raised; the city where he currently lived, in the house he had stepped out of that morning. Before he could protest, Alice had him by the hand again, leading him towards the main entrance, strolling across several acres of immaculately trimmed grass. At first, individual guests hurried past, gawking as they went. Howard heard shouting off to his right as several staff members emerged from the front door of the complex and sprinted across the large open lawn. Alice led him off to the left of the expansive front yard, past a row of trees, down a stone staircase to three large pools filled with water lilies and teaming with Koi fish. She released his hand and moved towards the water, her blonde ponytail bobbing, somehow unfazed by the swarm of rising voices.

"Alice...what's going on?" Howard asked, feeling the dread coiling back up inside his stomach. "Why is everyone so scared? What's happened?"

"Don't worry, Howard, everything is going to be fine," she said without turning. "It's Mother, Howard. She's calling to us. It's time to tell the world...you've got to keep digging. We all do."

Alice turned around, and the support beams holding up Howard's last shreds of sanity shattered inside his mind. The skin around Alice's face had been cut away in a large oval, leaving a layer of exposed muscle tissue and congealed blood. It felt like mercy as she turned away and walked smoothly past the pond toward the mountains behind the Biltmore House, their outlines blue in the distance.

"Alice!" he yelled, bounding forward as he moved past the water's calm surface.

He stopped, transfixed by his reflection in the closest pool. Other Howard grinned back at him, wearing a mask made from human skin. Howard dropped to his knees, craning his neck towards the water to see more clearly. The patch of freckles across the bridge of the nose was unmistakable. He wanted to scream, to wail and cry without reservation, but the most he could muster was a pained groan. Red and blue flashing lights reflected off every surface as the sound of police sirens filled the air. Howard's gaze drifted down to his clothes, and he saw himself clearly for the first time. He wore what might have once been a white robe, now ripped into stained strips of cloth, caked in dirt and filth. He had no shirt, only the remnants of tattered jeans. Blotches of dried mud covered his arms; the tips of his fingers were bloody and raw. His feet were shoeless, stained with more dried mud, peppered in scabs and fresh cuts. He looked up to see police officers shouting orders, guns drawn. Onlookers were pointing, many filming him on their phones, their looks of disgust matched only by his own.

Howard gave no resistance as the officers took hold of him

and hoisted him up, half dragging, half shoving him towards the back of an ambulance surrounded by a crescent of police cars. He was handcuffed to a stretcher as paramedics poked and prodded at him, their voices whispering a harsh cacophony of judgments and accusations. One of their hands rifled into a pocket of his robe and produced a small totem of magma, shining like black glass. *His totem; one of six. His favorite.* The sculpted woman was a wonder to behold in the reflected light. The dazzling eyes carved into her hair watched him expectantly. A sudden rage bubbled up inside Howard at the sight of his Goddess in the hands of another. He jerked forward as the handcuffs bit into his wrists, screaming and gnashing his teeth. The urge to hold her again was unbearable.

"Howard," an ethereal voice spoke inside his mind, emanating from the totem.

The woman, carved from ancient magma as black as onyx, spoke to him. It was the voice of Mother. She called to him, syrupy sweet in his ears, beckoning him from deep below. She was waiting for him, but her voice became blurred and watered down. There was a needle in his arm; something cold entered his veins. The medicine worked its way through his body, numbing him, detaching him from her comforting whisper. Howard sank into the stretcher, his muscles turning to boiled rubber. He felt Alice's face being peeled away like a sticky Band-Aid and heard one of the younger paramedics vomiting out the back of the ambulance, the contents of her stomach splattering on the pavement. He closed his eyes and wished for oblivion or even the slightest reprieve from his madness. The drugs finally took hold of him, and his wish was granted, his world fading to black.

"Howard," Mother's soft voice called. "Howard." The voice repeated, but the pitch of her voice was wrong. "Howard!" a man's voice shouted in the darkness, followed by an acrid smell that forced his eyes to bulge wide.

"There he is, rise and shine, boy," said a large man dressed in hospital scrubs, tall with meaty forearms and a slightly protruding belly. He was holding an open pack of smelling salts.

Howard was seated in a cushioned chair, arms bound in a straitjacket, ankle cuffed to one of the chair's wooden legs. The walls were decorated with replica works of art, an eclectic collection from different ages. Some were abstract or surreal, many of them disturbing. One painting showed a woman sleeping or perhaps dead, a small demon sitting on her chest as a black horse watched from the shadows. One he recognized as The Great Red Dragon and the Woman Clothed with the Sun. There were several shelves holding miniature replicas of statues, like Michelangelo's David, and busts of long-dead philosophers. A well-dressed man with oiled hair, round spectacles, and a groomed silver beard sat behind a large wooden desk, studying him thoughtfully.

Howard worked his neck, getting the feel of straps around the back of his head and a plastic shield covering the lower half of his face.

"No spitting today, eh?" the lumbering man asked.

"I'm sorry," Howard said, unsure of what he had done.

"Oh, he's sorry, is he?" the man laughed cruelly. "Hallelujah, Howard, I think you've turned a corner. Doctor Barlow, I'll draw up the discharge papers, eh?"

"Please, Miles, that's quite enough," Dr. Barlow chided. "Remorse is the guide to redemption." Dr. Barlow looked at Howard with kind eyes, though he had noticeable dark rings beneath them. "Howard, I can't tell you how pleased I am to see you so calm and coherent today. These last few weeks have been very difficult for you, to say the least."

"Weeks?" Howard asked, feeling his throat tighten.

"I know this is very confusing for you," Dr. Barlow said. "First, you must understand that you are safe under my care here at the Napa State Hospital in California. We have been forced to use heavy sedation to prevent you from hurting yourself or others. This is the calmest I've seen you in...weeks."

"Is that why I'm in this jacket?" Howard asked. "Did I hurt someone?"

"For the first several days after your arrival, you were

determined to dig into the floor of your room using your hands," Dr. Barlow explained.

Howard rubbed his fingers together inside cloth pouches, feeling ripped or missing fingernails. He shuddered, grateful he had no memory of his actions.

"Trying to dig your way to your *Mother*," Miles smirked.

Barlow gave him a sharp look of disapproval.

"Howard, while we have you so lucid, I'd like to pick up where we left off last time. Can you tell me about Elizabeth?" Dr. Barlow asked.

"Who?" Howard asked, unsure if Dr. Barlow was leading him through some sort of mind game.

Barlow breathed out a heavy sigh.

"Is that someone I hurt?" Howard asked.

"No, Howard, Elizabeth Allen is your wife."

"My wife," Howard said in disbelief. "I don't have a wife!"

"You do, Howard," Dr. Barlow continued. "You also have two children, ages four and two."

Howard squeezed his eye shut until they hurt, then kept pressing tighter, trying to force out an image of a family he couldn't remember. He snapped his head to the right, then left, a scream of frustration boiling up from inside.

"Howard, I need you to calm down," Dr. Barlow said in his calm, authoritarian voice. "We don't want to sedate now, do we?"

Howard squinted back, making a show of taking slow, deep breaths. Despite his fear and confusion, he knew he didn't want to return to a state of thoughtlessness.

"That's good," Dr. Barlow said, scribbling some notes on a pad at his desk. "That's very good. Now, I'm going to say several names, and I want you to tell me if they trigger any response, positive or negative."

Howard nodded his head in agreement.

"Clarissa Wolf," Dr. Barlow began. "Avery Hawkins. Enid Crosby. Julie Andrews."

Howard shook his head. *Were they old acquaintances? Childhood friends? Ex-girlfriends?*

"Their bodies were all found buried beneath your cabin in the woods," Miles cut in.

Victims then.

"Thank you, Miles," Dr. Barlow hissed, lips pursed in disapproval. "You may go now."

"But Doctor," Miles began.

Barlow raised a hand to silence him. "I must insist, Miles. I will be quite alright. Howard will be on his best behavior, isn't that right, Howard?"

Howard glanced at Miles, then back to Dr. Barlow. Howard nodded his agreement. Dr. Barlow gave Miles an insincere smile and gestured with his raised hand toward the door. Miles scowled down at Howard but turned without a rebuttal and left the room, pulling the door firmly shut.

"Please forgive his bluntness," Dr. Barlow said as he produced a key from inside his shirt, tied to a leather cord around his neck.

Barlow unlocked one of his desk drawers and opened it slowly, an adoring look on his face as he reached inside. He produced Howard's totem of Mother, setting it down on top of his desk with a weighty thud.

"Miles can't understand you, Howard." Dr. Barlow stroked the statue lovingly, gently caressing her hair. "Not like I can."

To his surprise, Howard felt no urge to jump for his idol, felt no need to tear his arms free of his restraints, and open Dr. Barlow's throat upon his gigantic desk. Instead, he felt calm; at peace; among friends.

"Can you...hear her?" Howard asked.

"Oh yes, Howard," Dr. Barlow said, removing his glasses as he leaned across the desk. "She speaks, but I do still have a question for you."

Howard leaned forward, a mirror image of his new conspirator. "What?" he asked, barely a whisper.

"How far, Howard?" Dr. Barlow asked. "How far must we dig?"

HELL CAN HAVE THE REST

C laire pushed the tip of the blade into soft flesh, applying steady pressure until she hit bone. Then, carefully, she extracted the thin piece of steel several inches before advancing back into the meat. Using a fork to hold everything very still, she made quick sawing motions until a flap of tender pork loin folded over onto her plate. Her date, Jeff, sat across from her at the dining room table, looking quite handsome in his tieless blue button-up. The smell of dinner filled her humble two-bedroom apartment, the roasted potatoes seasoned with a hint of rosemary, pairing nicely with the buttered snap peas and pan-fried mushrooms. Jeff swirled his red wine by the stem of his glass, looking at Claire like he could skip the meal right then and head straight to the bedroom for dessert. Claire, of course, would be damned if she let hours of preparation and cooking go to waste. She had worked up quite the appetite setting up the "kill room", as the local homicide detective Edward Lancaster liked to call it on the news. It took meticulous attention to detail, far more than most people realized, to ensure every drop of blood was accounted for. Men struggled, they twisted, and they splattered. *Proper preparation prevents poor performance.* That's what her father had loved to tell her. He had been right, of course. He had been right about a lot of things, actually. *Slow down and enjoy the ride.* That had been another good one. Besides, the food was delicious, and to be honest, Jeff was nice to look at. He had a soft golden tan, wavy brown hair, and a strong jawline. He looked fit but not so muscular that he couldn't be dragged or rolled over. Claire chose her targets carefully, just like she had been taught.

"So, Claire," Jeff began, a dreamy look in his eyes. "Tell me about your work."

Ugh, Claire thought. *The small talk*. She wished she had put more drugs in his wine.

"Well, Jeffry," she said, smiling as she popped a slice of tender meat into her mouth. "On paper, I've been a vet tech for the past four years. Continuous work history looks good to prying eyes."

Jeff seemed fascinated with her nonchalant tone. Some men found it alluring when they met a well-composed woman acting outside of her feminine wiles.

"Prying?" Jeff giggled. "Who's prying?"

Claire swallowed her savoring bite and flashed a predatory smile. "Well, Jeffry, technically speaking, you are. But I was referring to criminal profilers, for example. While I can't say I prescribe completely to the Crime Classification Manual, certain commonalities are shared between repeat violent crime offenders."

Jeff nodded his head, although he clearly didn't know what for.

"Offenders?" he asked.

"Serial killers, Jeffry."

Jeff raised his hands as if to tell her to stop the formalities. "Call me Jeff," he said, slurring the 'f' sound.

"Of course…Jeff," Claire said pleasantly.

Jeff's head nodded, and he jerked upright, displaying the panicked clarity one has when waking up after falling asleep in class. He shook away his fatigue and took another sip of his wine, quickly settling back into a lulled state. Claire stood and straightened her tight red mini skirt and decorative belt, then adjusted her bust to Jeff's wobbling enthusiasm. She cleared her throat and took several smooth strides past him, pausing when she got to her bedroom door. Jeff spun around, eyes struggling to stay open.

"Shall we?" she asked, licking her top lip. In truth, there was a spot of seasoning from dinner on her mouth, but to Jeff, she assumed it looked quite seductive.

Jeff gave a cheesy chin and rose, looking quite pleased with himself. Claire batted her dark green eyes and cracked the door, then slipped inside the darkened room, melting into the shadows. Jeff entered the room, fumbling with his belt, and pawed for the light switch. Claire stood to the right of the doorway, blade in hand, waiting patiently.

The lights cut on, and Jeff stared bug-eyed at the bedroom covered in sheets of painter's plastic. Claire sprang at Jeff, holding the blade flat and pointing at a slight angle. Severing a person's spinal cord was all about precision. The tip of the knife went in at the base of his skull but lodged firmly into one of his intervertebral discs, also known as the wrong spot. Jeff whipped around, both hands pawing at the protruding handle like he was doing some bizarre version of the macarena dance. Claire's smile soon vanished as Jeff gave a gurgled war cry and rushed toward her. Slick red hands found their way around her throat as he slammed her against the wall. *There's the real Jeff*, she thought—*the monster hiding inside the man*. Claire had no intention of dying in the grip of those bloody hands. Besides, she was already fishing out the switchblade stashed behind her belt. Jeff's outstretched arms left the rest of his body unguarded and Claire with two free hands. She plunged the second blade hard into the Axillary artery inside Jeff's left armpit, then yanked the upturned blade back towards herself. *That did the trick.* Jeff watched the blood gushing from beneath his arm in crimson spurts. *Jeff, the human fountain.* He turned, then pitched forward like a felled tree, striking the floor with a heavy thud and swishing of plastic. *Jeff, the dead man; hypoxia via exsanguination.*

Claire closed her eyes and smiled as if the sun of a new day was washing over her. The world was just a little bit brighter, a little bit safer. The moment of the kill was like a release of pressure, bringing an acute yet short-lived sense of relief. She opened her eyes and frowned down at the back of Jeff's slacks. Whenever authors or filmmakers tried to romanticize death, they usually left out the part where the guy voids his bowels. At any rate, the killing might be done, but the night was far from over. Being meticulous took time, and she wanted everything to be perfect when Detective Lancaster arrived at the scene the next day.

"Jeffry Duncan," Claire said, her voice growing cold as she gathered up the plastic sheets in one hand. "Your debt on Earth is paid. Hell can have the rest."

———————◆●◆———————

Edward Lancaster climbed to the top of an A-frame ladder, looking down onto his crime scene. The Broken Heart Killer, as the papers were dubbing him, brought his victims to a public area for display, arranged on the ground to be viewed from above like a three-dimensional painting. The sixth victim, Jeffry Duncan, had been placed on the grass so that he was bent down on one knee, looking up with a paper mâché rose in his hand, passing the flower into the waiting grasp of a department store mannequin. The mannequin was dressed in women's clothing and wore bright red lipstick as she smiled down on Mr. Duncan, one plastic hand pressed to her fake breast while Jeff's dead corpse reached for her affections. Edward ran his fingers down the back of his trimmed blonde hair and stewed on the latest images the killer had created. He was only twenty-six, but working the serial cases made him feel closer to fifty.

"Whatcha say, Ed?" Oscar Moreno asked from the base of the ladder.

Oscar was twenty-four, average height, and had thick, short dark hair combed over with the parting line buzzed in. He also had a half-inch scar etched into his right eyebrow, a reminder of his days in a gang as a kid. He had come a long way and made his parents damn proud.

"I say our killer is trying to say something beyond promoting a higher art form," Edward said, looking to meet his partner's eyes. "From what Mr. Duncan's coworkers said, he was pretty much an asshole."

"May he rest in peace," Oscar added hastily.

"Here's the thing," Edward continued. "At least two of our other victims were generally thought of the same way."

"You think the killer's looking to settle a score?" Oscar asked. "Or he's projecting childhood bullies onto the victims?"

"No, it feels more like he's teaching everyone a lesson. "Victims are presented like gentlemen," he studied Jeff Duncan and frowned. "We're still missing something."

"Detective, you should see this!" called one of the CSI techs.

A young woman was walking towards Edward as he came down the ladder, holding the paper flower in her hands.

"There's a message written inside the petals," she said, then read. "You look so lost, with hands on hips; I'll help you out, just read my lips."

Edward looked at the victim and then at the mannequin, studying its face.

"Holy hell," Edward said, the realization bubbling up from the depths of his subconscious. "The killer's a woman!"

"What makes you so sure?" asked Oscar, taking the note from the woman.

"Read my lips. My lips. The mannequin takes the place of the killer. We need to check that lipstick for DNA," Edward said excitedly.

"Oh shit," Oscar said, staring at the paper in his hands, his eyebrows almost at his hairline.

"What?" Edward asked, frowning.

"Ed, the paper used to make the flower," Oscar said, shaking his head. "It's a utility bill for *your* house."

———————◆●◆———————

Edward sat inside a local bar, tipping back a large stout as he watched sports highlights on TV. He was still trying to process the events of the day, surrounded by the sound of pool balls cracking as smoke clouds drifted up and collected in the rafters. Most of the patrons were blue-collar, although he spotted a few loosened ties at one of the tables.

"Mind if I sit?" a soft but confident voice asked from behind his left shoulder.

Edward turned and saw a beautiful young woman in nurse scrubs. She had short brown hair in a shaggy bob. Emerald green eyes looked him over as she slid the chair out beside him, then slipped into the seat without waiting for his approval.

"Oh, yeah, of course," he said after the fact.

He noticed a stain of blood on the woman's left sleeve.

"I've heard of rough bedside manners, but jeez," Edward asked with a grin.

She gave a sarcastic smile. "No," she said, embellishing the word. "I actually work for a vet. I was going to change first, but I thought screw it; maybe a little blood will keep the creepers away."

"Sorry to disappoint," Edward grinned again, lifting his beer in a salute. *Damn, he was grinning a lot.*

"I figured you can't be too bad with that badge," she said coolly, pointing at his hip.

Edward had come straight to the bar from the crime scene, not in a rush to head home after the note.

"Very observant," he said, trying to look impressed. "Eddie," he said, extending a hand.

"Claire," she replied, taking his hand in a firm grip. "You wouldn't happen to be working, *the murders*," she whispered.

Edward put a finger to his lips and smiled. "Don't tell anyone. I'm too tired for autographs." *Damn, he was grinning again.*

They talked about anything and everything late into the evening. Close to ten, she checked her phone and grimaced.

"Ugh, I should be going. I've got to be back at the clinic early tomorrow."

She took a bar napkin, wrote down her number, folded it into a heart, and slid it across the counter. "We should do this again sometime."

"Definitely," he said.

"It was nice to meet you, Eddie," she said, smiling.

"You too, Claire," he grinned back for the hundredth time.

He stuffed the paper in his pocket and watched her go, already thinking about the next time he might see her again.

Claire stood outside by the curb, looking up at the stars. She imagined Eddie standing beside her, kissing her in the middle of the sidewalk, forcing people to go around them. *Why was she being so reckless? You don't develop feelings for the person wanting to put you away.* Yet there was something about him that drew her in. There was a goodness to him, a kindness that she trusted. She could make him understand. They could even work together one day, ridding the world of the real monsters...either behind bars or beneath the dirt. *He wants to see me again*, she thought, strolling down the dimly lit alley beside the bar. She retrieved the bookbag full of her tools for the night's job. She checked her blades, and counted several rolls of duct tape and two packs of painter's plastic. Her target was six blocks away, but she didn't mind the walk. It would give her time to plan her next date with Eddie. She would be seeing him a lot sooner than he imagined.

OUR FATHER

"Our Father, who art in Heaven, hallowed be Thy name," I said, placing a hand on little Elenore's forehead.

Beads of sweat prickled her skin as she whimpered and strained against the firm grip of her Uncle Harry and older brother Simon. Elenore's mother, Judith stood perched in the corner, a hand over her mouth in a vain attempt to stop her sobbing. I had been summoned the week before, but heavy snowfalls delayed my carriage by three days. The house was part of a small community twenty miles east of Lake Eerie.

Judith's letter had spoken of strange happenings. Small animals had been found ripped to pieces, and unearthly sounds were heard in the late hours of the night. Elenore had been discovered on several occasions, standing in her sleep robes in the woods, staring out and uttering unintelligible whispers into the dark. Judith's husband, Jonathan, had died in the house the year prior. He had been a cruel man by all accounts. Although he had rid the family of his foul presence by suicide, Judith now worried that his spirit still haunted the home. Worse yet, she feared his evil presence had somehow infected their little girl. Judith's letter to the church had requested an exorcism, and right away.

I'll tell you a secret now. I have performed exorcisms to dispel demons, yes, but most of the time, I'm dispelling demons of the mind instead. At times, a theatric reciting of prayer is all it takes to chase the phantoms from our lives. A haunted home may simply be the product of haunted memories.

Because of my tardiness, we had begun late at night. The

snow had also resumed, shining from the light of a full moon.

"You have to let me go!" Elenore screamed, thrashing wildly as the two large men struggled beneath her small frame.

"Hold fast!" I commanded them, growing frustrated at their half-attempt to contain the child.

I turned away, digging in my bag to retrieve my crucifix, when I heard Judith scream. Harry stumbled back, gripping his abdomen as streams of blood wove through his clutching fingers. Elenore was gone from the bed, replaced by what I could only describe as a wolf-like beast standing on its haunches, dressed in her clothes. The creature had Simon by the throat, its powerful jaws ripping and tearing as blood sprayed in all directions. Without thinking, I reached forward to pull her away but was met with a slash across my forearm that sent me stumbling backward. Elenore turned to face me, her chest expanding as her clothing stretched and split. Simon's blood oozed from her gaping maw.

To my shame, all my trinkets and amulets meant absolutely nothing at that moment. I turned from the bestial form that had once been sweet Elenore and fled for my life. Her mother's piercing cries of agony followed me down the stairs as if accusing me and branding me a coward. Still, I ran. I gave no thought to prayers, only the notion that I needed my breath to keep running. I heard the shattering of glass, which must have been the second-story window. There was no looking back, only the pursuit of a safe haven. A primal urge had awakened in me, the flight of prey as it leaps and bounds, darting away as the predator closes in.

I scrambled through snow drifts, ignoring the creeping cold working its way up my legs, gripping me like frozen weights. A hidden root caught my right boot, and I dove forward as my arms disappeared into a small hill of finely powdered snow. I dragged myself up and limped on, a new stab of searing pain throbbing in my right thigh. I was moving too slowly, and my sense of direction was working as well as a broken compass. Fresh curtains of falling snow glistened in the moonlight, obscuring my path. I entered a clearing and stopped running so I could listen. A calm silence had settled over the woods, save for the savage beating of my heart. A soft crunching sent me spinning, frantically looking for forms within the shadows, seeing them everywhere around me. The pain in my forearm was making me feel sick.

A single wolf emerged from the tree line. The moon reflected off the snowy clearing, giving me enough light to see it was no ordinary wolf. Pieces of patterned fabric clung to its fur, the remains of Elenore's dress. My breath caught in my throat as the beast stood on its hind legs. My blood turned to ice water as more of the creatures came into the clearing, all standing and walking, thick, wiry hair covering their bodies. It was a pack of cursed children converging upon me.

"God, help me!" I cried, falling to my knees.

"Our father," Elenore said in a grating voice.

"Our father," the others repeated.

They gathered around me, a crescent of terrible forms, chanting over and over. "Our father. Our father."

Elenore drew closer still, so close I could smell the blood on her breath.

"You have the right bloodline, Father," she said as drops of scarlet fell from her mouth, staining the snow red.

The burning in my arm had spread into my chest. The woods appeared to be getting brighter, the shadows melting away as my senses sharpened, drawing in strange smells and sounds of the forest. Elenore's lips curled into a grotesque smile.

"The change has begun," she said with troubling satisfaction.

The circle closed as my arms and legs locked up in violent spasms.

"Our father," their voices echoed inside my head.

I tried to scream, but a howling cry pierced the night instead. A primal chorus rang out in response.

I'll never forget the first night of my change, as the children's voices welcomed me as the leader of their pack.

"Our father."

III. SATIRE

"Satire can always be found everywhere. A people without love for satire is a dead people." -Dario Fo

APPLES TO ASHES, DIRT TO DUST

"This war has been raging for fifty years!" William Weiner bellowed to his dozen children, holding up an exquisite Red Delicious apple. "My brother, that bony old bastard Jacob, thinks his orchard is better than ours!"

There was a rumble of disdain from his sons and daughters, ranging from preteens all the way to adults with children of their own.

"He thinks that *his family* is better than ours!" William said, his puffy cheeks turning the same shade as the fruit in his hand. "This season, our town will recognize the Hard Apples Orchard as the best damn orchard in Washington State!"

Tommy Doolittle, a small-time reporter, watched in amazement as William's words whipped them into greater heights of anger and pride. Tommy jotted down notes in his little black notebook, already developing his story for the local paper. *War of the Weiners*, he thought, rolling the title around in his head. *The Weiner Wars? Maybe it was best to stick with an apple theme*, he decided. *Two Bad Apples*, he mused, pleased with himself. The Weiner family was something of a town attraction in its own right. Two brothers, William, and Jacob Weiner, had been at each other's throats long before Tommy had been born. They were competitive in all things, whether it be spawning children, owning the best orchard, or even the pronunciation of their surname. While William proudly aligned himself with the tried-and-true Oscar Myer *Weiner*, Jacob insisted the name was pronounced "whiner" and had complained about such a fact for over thirty years. Continuing another family tradition, William's group of Weiners all dressed in blue overalls. It reminded Tommy of a military uniform or a type of cult apparel. Jacob's side wore yellow overalls, which were most offensive to the eyes but made them unmistakable during the harvest season.

"Remember!" William warned, "There will be no consorting with the enemy," he shook his head. "No discussing of family business, and absolutely *no* hanky-panky."

Tommy found William's last remark most disturbing with its implications, seeing how both sides of the Weiners were family. William's oldest son, Dolph Weiner, stepped forward beside his father. He was stocky, with a dark tan, minus a light-skinned imprint left by the sunglasses he wore every day.

"We made a pact over ten years ago that no one would try to build within the fifty-yard strip separating our two orchards," Dolph said. "Year after year, they moved the line, forcing us to do the same on our side. This year, only ten feet separate us, and I can guarantee you they will take it to five. It's up to us to beat them back."

"Stay firm," William warned, "and stay focused. We only have two more weeks until the farmers market, and we plan to unveil our brand-new apple variety we've been developing for years. Get to it, everyone!"

The gathering started to disperse, with several individuals cracking open beers in the middle of the town square. Tommy glanced at his watch, which read nine fifty-five in the morning, made a few more notes, and headed across town to hear Jacob speak.

———————◆●◆———————

Jacob had overtaken a small pavilion on the east end of their small town. A banner hung proudly declaring "Big Apples Orchard".

Yellow overalls were all gathered together like bundles of giant bananas.

"My sons and daughters!" Jacob shouted in a dry, nasally voice. "This year, we're going to show this town why we are the number one producer of apples and apple products this side of the cascade mountains!"

A cheer went up, adding to the more positive energy coming from this half of the Weiner family.

"Now, before we go over preparations for this year's market, I have a very special announcement. Musical entertainment for the Big Apples Orchard this year will be provided by..." he let the silence stretch, relishing in the anxious pacing of his thirteen children. "Washington native, Sir Mix-a-Lot!"

Tommy noticed the blank slate of the younger generations' faces, mixed with the nostalgic smiles of the older siblings. Jacob's family was known for their affinity for celebrity guests at their events, while William tried to unveil the "next big thing" if such a term was even applicable in the apple world.

Jacob waved his oldest daughter Lundy up beside him. Her bust was pressed to the forefront in her tight set of overalls, the pant legs cut off to make frayed shorts. Two large braids of thick red hair made her look eerily similar to a grown-up version of the Wendy's restaurant logo.

"Last year, William and his family threw several limp accusations towards us about causing damage to his saplings or roughing up a few of his children. Please show some discretion this year. We don't need the bad press."

Tommy knew she didn't condemn the behavior but only expected them not to get caught doing it.

"And if a couple of his trees fall down in the middle of the night," she continued, "well, beavers can be bad this time of year."

Jacob gave a toothy grin and nodded his approval. Tommy looked around and noticed several of the younger boys slip away and make their way toward a thick patch of woods with bookbags slung over their shoulders, looking guilty as sin. Always one for a story, he followed them from a distance, struggling to track them, even with their yellow overalls. There was a commotion from the brush further to the left, and several boys wearing blue overalls emerged. Tommy saw a few fist bumps exchanged and heard the clap of a crisp high-five. Their group became six and continued their trek further into the forest. Tommy paused, realizing he didn't want to be seen slinking after some young boys into the woods, and figured, *how much trouble could they really get into?*

Two weeks later, the town was buzzing with activity during the farmer's market. Booths of local vegetables, baked goods, flowers, tools, crafts, and trinkets had been set up on a strip of land directly between the two opposing orchards. At one end of the field, a giant stand had been erected for Hard Apples Orchard, and at the other end stood two slightly smaller booths on either side of a long wooden stage. A banner stretching the two smaller booths read "Big Apples Orchard". Both sides of the family had been passing out their particular brand of ciders, giving out free samples with the hopes of expanding their hard-won customer bases. It became clear to Tommy that the town was well divided between the two houses, groups of folks generally sticking to one orchard or the other. A round stage with a stand and speakers was set up smack in the center of the neutral land for the mayor's office to make announcements. Whooping and hollering at such events was expected, but the noise had become louder and more frequent until Tommy realized a growing panic had overtaken the entire event. To his surprise, the six boys from the woods appeared on the mayor's stage, with their leader taking hold of the microphone.

"Excuse me," the young boy said. "My name is Richard Weiner, and I have something I need to say."

The crowd quieted slightly, and William and Jacob moved in closer from each side of the field. Jacob watched his young boy with a look of grumpy confusion.

"The fighting between the Weiners has grown out of hand to the point that this small town can barely contain it," Richard said. "Can't you all see how divided we are? Can't you both see that the kids don't want any part of your war?" he asked his father and uncle, making both men stiffen with indignity. "We don't even know why we're supposed to hate each other!" Richard spat. "To promote peace and help expand your minds, we've infused both of the Weiner's cider with a few special ingredients, grown on the land shared between our two families. You're all drinking a highly fermented mixture of the finest apples infused with several experimental strains of spliced magic mushrooms!"

Tommy dropped his cup of cider as the town erupted into a full-on panic.

"He's trying to kill us all!" William shouted, pointing in Jacob's direction.

William hurled a shiny red apple at Jacob. It sailed through the air, narrowly striking him in the face.

"To arms!" Jacob cried, filling each hand with a Granny Smith.

The families, including the townsfolk, divided like a massive game of dodgeball. The two orchards quickly devolved into a war zone as nature's forbidden fruits became nature's projectile weapons. Tommy tried his best to think of something he could say on stage to stop the fighting, but he was still "tripping balls", as the kids liked to say. The blue and yellow overalls danced merrily about him, whispering to him to find and wear a pair himself.

"Wait!" Dolph roared from the center stage, joined by Lundy close at his side.

To Tommy's giggling joy, the town calmed down.

"The boys are right," Dolph continued. "It's time to settle things once and for all, the old-fashioned way, the way the Weiners did over a hundred years ago."

Lundy produced two shovels and tossed them down to stick in the dirt.

"Willy and Jacob, you know the rules," Lundy shouted. "You each dig a hole. The first one to stop loses. The last man standing wins, and his orchard is declared the best. The entire town supports him, and the loser can grow tomatoes for all we care."

"Despicable fruit," Dolph added.

"Will you both agree?" Lundy demanded.

The whole town had gone silent, except for a few screamers, as they studied William and Jacob intensely.

"Of course, I will!" William declared, his face beet red.

"I'd be happy to beat you off our land!" Jacob taunted.

"Then it's settled," Dolph proclaimed, "start digging!"

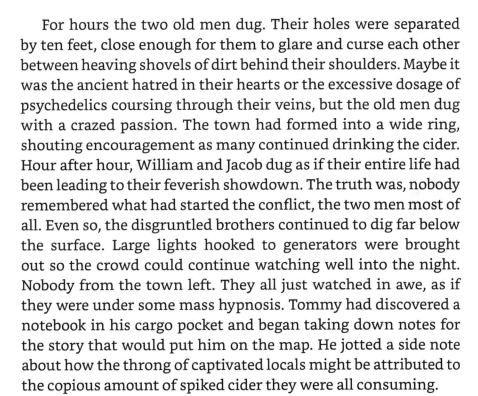

For hours the two old men dug. Their holes were separated by ten feet, close enough for them to glare and curse each other between heaving shovels of dirt behind their shoulders. Maybe it was the ancient hatred in their hearts or the excessive dosage of psychedelics coursing through their veins, but the old men dug with a crazed passion. The town had formed into a wide ring, shouting encouragement as many continued drinking the cider. Hour after hour, William and Jacob dug as if their entire life had been leading to their feverish showdown. The truth was, nobody remembered what had started the conflict, the two men most of all. Even so, the disgruntled brothers continued to dig far below the surface. Large lights hooked to generators were brought out so the crowd could continue watching well into the night. Nobody from the town left. They all just watched in awe, as if they were under some mass hypnosis. Tommy had discovered a notebook in his cargo pocket and began taking down notes for the story that would put him on the map. He jotted a side note about how the throng of captivated locals might be attributed to the copious amount of spiked cider they were all consuming.

Sometime around two in the morning, the cider had run dry, and the crowds were starting to disperse. William and Jacob had disappeared from sight, although an occasional shower of dirt was still heaved up from the shadowy depths. There was a cry of alarm as the ground began to grumble and moan. Then, there was a terrible sound of rock tearing as the earth heaved and shook. Muffled shouting escaped the holes right before two gushing columns of oil shot into the sky. The sons and daughters of William and Jacob Weiner moved in as close as they dared, trying to locate their fathers, though the outcome seemed grim.

The Weiner children all glanced around at one another, their overalls soaked and stained black by the oily shower. Sensing the climax to his big story, Tommy crept forward as he scribbled into his notepad. With the yellow and blue of their overalls gone, the children seemed to see one another as one giant pack of Weiners for the first time. Dolph and Lundy were the first to realize the monetary value of their fathers' deaths. Several excited whispers passed between them, and it surprised Tommy to see their fingers interlace in an overly familiar display of affection.

The bodies of William and Jacob Weiner were recovered two days later, but nobody seemed much to care. The remaining Weiners were rich. Word soon got out that Dolph and Lundy were planning their wedding, and the official color for the new family overalls was changed to green. Eventually, the last name Weiner was dropped, and they became the Winners by a majority vote. The orchards were cleared away, and the land was soon turned into the Winner's Family Oil Field. Tommy tried to explain to Dolph that Lundy was his cousin and their marriage was taboo, but Dolph wouldn't hear a word of it, citing they had decided to become cousins twice removed, making the marriage "legit". Tommy further explained that's not how those things worked, but Dolph just wished him well and sent him home with two free gallons of the famous Winner's Mushroom Cider. Once he was back in his office, Tommy took out his notebook and got started on his first book, "From Weiners to Winners".

DISGRUNTLED

John had great big waterproof boots on that came up to his knees. This was especially important when walking through an inch of human blood. John pushed the handle of his squeegee across the marble floor of the empty twenty by twenty-foot room in ever-shrinking circles, making sure to get every last drop down the drain. To be wasteful would ultimately lead to more work, which made John wince at the thought. He still had the heavy fellow in the corner to deal with before his evening could come to a close. The man, Tanner or Conner, *something with 'er*, was dead as a spent battery. An all too familiar look of horror was frozen on his face as if he had died from fright, although they both knew that fear was not what had killed him. John opened the drain and removed the collection jar, making sure to screw the lid on tightly.

When someone had to dispose of as many bodies as John did, efficiency was the key. *Work smarter, not harder*; his father had always told him. Smarter meant cremating the bodies, but the incinerator was on the fritz, and the repair man couldn't get parts ordered for at least a week. It looked like an old-fashioned burial in the woods would round out his abysmal evening. There was High Peaks Wilderness to the west or Dix Mountain Wilderness to the east. John's shoulders slumped so low he could have passed for a hunchback. *Well, at least he was already wearing the boots for it.*

It was well past one in the morning when John pulled back up to the gothic revival-style mansion nestled deep in the Adirondack mountains of upstate New York. Several towers peaked with spires stabbed up at the sky, adorned with stone gargoyles and weeping angels. He could barely feel his hands, and he was quite certain the tip of his nose had dropped off at some point earlier in the night. He tossed his muddy shovel into one of the outdoor utility sheds and kicked the door closed.

"And that," said John, "is that."

Like a mantra, he found the phrase comforting, letting him know he had completed a task, even if many more awaited him the next day. Inside the giant manor, the temperature wasn't much warmer than outside. The hearth lay bare, cleaned, and polished like most of the cold marble flooring. The lights were kept intentionally low, causing John to squint constantly to distinguish shapes and shadows. A black silhouette perched precariously along the lip of the vaulted ceiling suddenly skittered to the left, then poured down one of the four ornate pillars toward the floor like a waterfall of darkness.

John cleared his throat. "Master," he said towards the darkness.

"Johhhhn," came a rich Romanian accent.

Lord Marius Dalca Cojocaru materialized before John, double-chinned and filling out his velvet coat more like an overstuffed pillow, with tall spidery legs jutting out from beneath a puff of rich fabric.

"You have returned quite late, Johhhhn," Lord Cojocaru lamented, saying his name like a drawn-out yawn, stroking at his fine black mustaches.

"Master," John bowed, hiding the annoyance on his face. "I've traveled quite far today, both in finding your meal and disposing of the remains."

"Did I not pay to install the kiln?"

"Master, the kiln is the oven for your pottery. The cremation oven has been broken for quite some time."

"Well, then fix it, Johhhhn. I expect you to handle my day-to-day affairs!"

John ground his teeth together, making sure to keep a calm face.

"And it is my honor to do so. Perhaps if we were to get some type of internet service…" Lord Cojocaru threw his hands up and made a face like he had just tasted lemons.

"…or some kind of telephone, then I could at least…"

"Bah!" Lord Cojorau interrupted. "These modern trappings of the world, Johhhhn, they are like a *prison*. We do not need them."

"This house is a prison," John mumbled.

"What is that, Johhhhn?" Lord Cojocaru asked, cupping a hand behind one ear. "What is it, you say? Do you not know I have expert hearing? Do you not know I hear your every move? You pass gas; I shall hear it. You make number two; I shall hear the splash." John made a face. "You have happy time alone; I shall…"

"Ok, Ok, I get it," John said, exasperated.

How long had Cojocaru promised John wealth, power, and eternal life? Instead, he dusted unused furniture, cleaned empty hallways, and was an accomplice to murder for the world's laziest vampire.

"Do you want me to starve, Johhhhn? Is that why you are taking so long?" Lord Cojocaru asked, turning away dramatically.

"Master, it's two hours to Albany, two and a half to Monreal, plus the pain of border crossing. Plattsburgh is a bit over an hour, but you said they taste bad."

"There is something wrong with the blood!" Lord Cojocaru insisted.

"My point Master, some round trips are around five hours. Then, add the time it takes to find the victim, to get them from the point of greeting to inside the trunk. You can transform into a bat Master. Perhaps you could fly to them on occasion," John said, trying not to sound too hopeful.

Lord Cojocaru's head snapped back towards James, and his eyes narrowed. "Do I need to flap-flap over there, Johhhhn? Do you think I need the exercise?"

"No, my master, you have the body of a…predator." *Like a fat house cat*, John thought.

"That is right," Lord Cojocaru said, chest puffed out. "And if you ever hope to become my equal, you will do as I command. Oh, and be sure to clean my ledge tomorrow. I almost slipped in all the dust up there."

"Master, that's like thirty feet off the ground," John said.

Lord Cojocaru made a show of his fangs. "Clean it, Johhhhn."

"Yes, Master," John said, bowing again.

John leaned against the counter at his umpteenth bar in Montreal, looking for Lord Cojocaru's next meal. He wanted to find someone lighter and easier to drag; his lower back was acting up again. He spotted a striking young woman, in her late twenties-early thirties, at the far end of the bar top. She was playing with a strand of fiery red hair, twirling it around her finger before letting it spring back into place. John considered himself moderately handsome, but this woman was well out of his league. She cut her eyes in his direction, and he felt a sudden flush on his cheeks. *Too pretty*, he told himself. *People always go looking for the pretty ones.*

There was another woman, face flattened against a jukebox in the corner, still trying to pour a beer into the corner of her mouth. That's the one. He took a step in her direction and almost ran right into the redhead.

"Drink?" the woman asked, pushing a cold beer into his hands. "I'm Eabha."

John caught a rich Irish tone in her voice, adding an additional level of allure.

"John," he smiled, eyes darting over to the jukebox.

"Is she with you, John?" Eabha asked, eyebrows raised.

John caught himself from spitting beer down the front of Eabha's shirt, coughing at the burning in his nose.

"God no, I just uh," John looked at Eabha, watching him, a curious smile on her face like she might actually be interested. "I've got a big party to get to later. Kiefer Sutherland's got a thing."

"You know Kiefer?" she asked, eye narrowing.

"He slept with my cousin a few times," John replied with one of his go-to lines. "There's going to be loads of people there. Booze. Drugs. Whatever you're into. He's got a house down in the Adirondacks. There are always talent scouts at these things. You could always come check it out if you like."

"Impressive, she mused. "But it just so happens, I've got a celebrity party of my own to attend here locally."

"Really, who?" John asked.

"Rachel. McAdams."

"What, no way! I love her," he said.

"She's got all the booze and twice the drugs. What do you say?" Eabha asked.

"Wait a minute," John said, recognizing his own tactics. "Are you trying to lure me?"

"Are you trying to lure *me*?" she fired back.

"Oh my God," John laughed. "What are the chances? I had no idea there were others like me out there."

The words spilled from John's mouth, telling Eabha about Lord Cojocaru and the endless misery of chores he performed in the giant empty mansion. She let him blather, nodding or shaking her head as she observed him.

"But, I mean, you know what it's like, right?" John finally asked. "I'm sure you've got loads of stories to tell."

"John," she said slowly. "Are you a familiar? Are you Lord Cojocaru's sla...I mean, non-paid servant?"

"Yeah, I, uh, take care of the estate, fetch the meals, standard stuff, right?"

"No, John, You poor misguided creature. I catch my own prey. A true vampire lives for the hunt."

"You're a *vampire*?" he asked, mouthing the word. "Oh man, this is so embarrassing. I'm so sorry. I would never try to, you know, seduce or, uh, lure such a lovely and capable vampire such as yourself to her death. I have nothing but admiration for your kind. That's why I do what I do. To one day become one...of you."

"You were being seductive?"

John blushed, trying to clear his throat. "So, you really don't have people for this?" He waved a hand around the bar.

"What kind of lazy ass vampire would I be if I sent a human to get my food every night."

"Exactly!" John shouted. "That's what I'm always saying. Who does that, right? I just don't have any familiar friends for reference, you know."

"Look, John, I like you, and perhaps I even feel a bit sorry for you."

John let his head drop.

"No, no, not like that," she assured him. "I just mean Lord Cojocaru sounds like a real prick."

"Well, now that I've seen what a real vampire looks like, I realize I've been missing out. I'd kill to be your familiar. Literally."

Eabha smiled. "Perhaps, we can come to some sort of... arrangement."

———————◆●◆———————

When John walked through the front doors of Lord Cojocaru's estate, he was waiting in the main hall, arms crossed, a scowl painted on his face.

"Where have you been, Johhhhn?" he growled. "Without your presence, I was forced to feed on several raccoons. One got loose and completely destroyed the kitchen and downstairs bathroom, which you will, of course, be cleaning."

"You know," Eabha said as she sauntered in behind John. "I rather like the place. Much bigger than my flat up north."

Lord Cojocaru startled, then smoothed down his mustaches. "Johhhhn, who is this lovely creature? If I had known you were bringing company, I would have surely been more...patient."

"Did you know Cojocaru means sheepskin?" Eabha asked.

"It most certainly does not!" Lord Cojocaru protested.

"Yeah, it does," John chimed in. "We Googled it...with the internet."

"How dare you speak to me this way, Johhhhn!" Lord Cojocaru shrieked, baring his fangs.

John returned a toothy smile, showing off his new set of fangs back to his previous master.

"How...I," Lord Cojocaru began, then his eyebrows raised with realization. "You!" he pointed at Eabha. "How dare you turn my familiar!"

"How dare you treat me the way you did!" John shouted. "And it's John, not Johhhhn!" he turned to look at Eabha, who nodded her approval. "There's going to be some changed around here," he continued. Eabha will be moving in with us."

"She most certainly will not," Lord Cojocaru said indignantly.

"We could always stake your heart tonight," she offered.

Lord Cojocaru swallowed.

"Now be a lamb and fetch us something to eat," Eabha said.

"And that," said John, "is that."

IV. SCIENCE FICTION

*"Science fiction encourages
us to explore... all the futures,
good and bad, that the
human mind can envision." -
Marion Zimmer Bradley*

THE CAPTIVE

Sunday, May 10, 2020

My name is Dr. Peter Morris. While I have signed dozens of non-disclosure agreements during my time at Site X, promising not to talk about what goes on here, I feel compelled to record the treatment of prisoners under the supervision of Lieutenant Colonel Hughes.

As for our exact location, I could not say. Once a week, I take a two-hour helicopter ride from a private airport outside of Las Vegas, and the craft itself has no windows. Perhaps they fly around in circles to make sure I'm thoroughly confused, or maybe our location really is two hours away. Once we land, the platform lowers beneath the ground on a giant elevator, and I do not depart until the roof above has closed.

Over the last six months, my role has been divided between an attending physician and "good cop" to Hughes's "bad". Site X is home to prisoners, deemed the worst of the worst by Hughes, although I suspect he uses that rationale to justify interrogations that have more in common with medieval torture. At the end of this week, I will take my journal with me on the return trip to submit as evidence against Hughes and anyone else with a hand in this operation.

Monday, May 11, 2020

Today's interrogations began with a new prisoner, who I will refer to as Mr. Blue, due to the blue jumpsuit he wore while strapped to a steel chair in the center of the room. Mr. Blue looked to be in his thirties, handsome with dark hair and heterochromia, one eye being green and the other brown. He was clean-shaven and had a thin pink scar, like a forking river of blood, winding from the tip of his chin to the right corner of his mouth. He already had several bruises on his face and collarbone, and I suspect more beneath the jumpsuit. Prisoners sometimes came to us this way, already having visited several facilities before making their way to Site X.

In our very first session, Hughes did not ask Mr. Blue a single question, yet he burned his left arm with heated wire, shocked him with a Taser, and deprived him of oxygen multiple times by holding a sheet of painter's plastic over his face. Unlike the last two men sitting in that chair, Mr. Blue did not cry out in pain or beg for mercy. Later that night, on my way back to my quarters, I passed several sealed rooms, hearing the moans of some tortured soul. I passed Darren in the hall as I neared the end. He cleans the facility. The water in his mop bucket was stained red with blood. He smiled as he wished me a good night.

Tuesday, May 12, 2020

Mr. Blue was strapped to a gurney while Hughes asked him questions in several languages, including French, Arabic, and Russian. I'll give it to Hughes, I figured him a dumb, blunt instrument, but he's far more intelligent than I imagined. It makes him more dangerous, though, and I regret underestimating him and what he's capable of. Hughes asked Mr. Blue things like his name, where he came from, and what his intentions were…all questions were met with the same blank, unwavering stare. His silence led to continued electrocutions. After Mr. Blue passed out from several minutes of the treatment, I was charged with reviving him.

I have heard Hughes using terms like "useless" and "disposal" often. Once Hughes gets into a mental state like that, a prisoner's time with us does not last much longer. I wheeled Mr. Blue back to his room, flanked by four armed guards. The men helped hoist Mr. Blue from the chair and set him down on his bed, resting his back against the wall. Mr. Blue watched me with his different-colored eyes as they set him down. The entire thing felt bizarre and unnerving. There was no hate or judgment in his stare. It was as if he was trying to figure me out just by looking at me. It made me feel vulnerable somehow, and I soon looked away. When I dared another glimpse back, his eyes were closed, and he had reassumed his typical meditative pose.

Five more days, and I'll be out of this hell hole. The only redeeming quality of Site X is that the food is pretty good. Tonight, I had steak medallions with seasoned potatoes and vegetables. The prisoner's food is terrible and meager by design. Mr. Blue has not been fed for the last two days.

Wednesday, May 13, 2020

I would describe Hughes as something of a master torturer, but he truly excels at the practice of waterboarding. During an evening meal, he told me offhand that he perfected his technique in Iraq. Two months ago, we had been interrogating a man named Hasim. Hughes had kept Hasim near the point of drowning for almost an hour. Hasim had been in tears, bubbling like a small child. That man had been truly broken, giving names and locations to places I had never even heard of. As we tortured Mr. Blue in the same fashion, I was overcome with the strangest sensation. As I looked down at the black cloth covering his face while two assistants poured the water, I could feel Mr. Blue staring straight at me. Then, I could see his face, as if the cloth wasn't even there. As gallon after gallon of water was poured over his mouth, he watched me with an unblinking stare.

I still couldn't see the cloth, making me think I was going mad. I discretely removed myself from the room to escape Mr. Blue's haunting stare. With my eyes closed and back pressed against the wall, I took several deep breaths to allow my heart to slow down. The door to the interrogation room opened, and one of the guards stuck his head into the hallway. He told me that Hughes wanted me back in the room. Mr. Blue was ready to talk. When I re-entered the room, Mr. Blue watched me as his chest heaved with effort. I noticed his hands shaking and realized that his silent act had been hiding the fact that his time had been agony. Maybe it was mental fortitude or sheer stubborn will, but his body was starting to fail him, resulting in a final act of compliance. Something made me think he was really just playing for more time.

The prisoner, Mr. Blue, became Salem Alden. He claimed that his memories were fragments and that if he could eat and sleep at least one night without torment, he may be able to remember more. Hughes had laughed in his face but agreed without a trace of conviction in his belief. Salem looked at me as he offered thanks. I did not stay to watch him eat.

Thursday, May 14, 2020

I'm writing this early morning. I wish I had someone to talk to, but I fear what they would think. I woke up, or became aware I was awake, while standing in front of my bathroom mirror. The front of my t-shirt was soaking wet, and a broken drinking glass was lying in pieces on the hard tile of the bathroom floor in a small pool of water. I can only assume I cut my finger on a piece of that glass and was using the bloody tip of my finger to write messages on the mirror. It was hard to read, with many of the smudges looking crude and freeform, like I couldn't decide if I was writing or drawing pictures like some ancient caveman. I could make out one word in blood, sending me into a fit of shaking and feeling like a wild beast was chewing on my guts. The word "HELP" reflected back at me, still wet with the freshness of its writing. It's got to be the stress of this place. I've ignored the pleading of my heart for too long, and my subconsciousness has started to rebel. Three more days until the helicopter arrives. I can do this.

The interrogation today was a surreal nightmare. The exchange between Salem and Hughes took a hard turn into the realm of the bizarre. Hughes produced a detailed map of our galaxy and placed a laser pointer in Salem's fingers, though his arms were still strapped to the steel chair. Hughes commanded Salem to point at the location of ship formations, then asked for exact numbers and payload capabilities. To my surprise, Salem pointed to the moons Titan and Phoebe orbiting Saturn. Salem was speaking to Hughes, but I couldn't hear a thing, as if the volume of the world had been decreased to zero. I felt ill. Salem's multicolored eyes kept flickering over to watch me, filling me with increasing dread. A gentle whisper filled my ears, telling me Hughes was going to kill me. It didn't feel like internal dialogue, more like a scientist stating a fact about the universe. I looked to Hughes, but he was too absorbed with Salem, drinking up every word like an alcoholic trapped in a wine cellar. The rest of the interrogation was a haze. I can't shake the words in my head or the growing suspicion that Salem was the one who spoke them.

Friday, May 15, 2020

Morris, it is Salem. Please forgive me. I write these words with your hand. We are both in danger. I have said too much to Hughes, and you have heard too much to be allowed to leave. You will be dead before Sunday, and I soon after. Hughes will wait until he can confirm the information I have given. He will not be happy when he discovers I have lied. There is a way we may survive, but it will require trust. I have looked into your mind. You are a good man, but you do not have the strength to save yourself. I can help you. Tonight, you must open your mind to me. You must willfully surrender so that our minds may join. I am sorry for attempting to control you earlier without your permission. I am desperate. Tonight, as you lay in bed, repeat these words. I give you control. Let it be your mantra as you drift to sleep, and I will do the rest. Please trust me, Peter. It's the only way.

I woke with a pen in my hand and the journal entry above written in handwriting I don't recognize. What the hell is happening to me? Have I suffered a total psychotic break? Yesterday, Salem and Hughes had talked about secret military formations out near the moons of Saturn, for God's sake. Hughes hadn't even seemed fazed by the conversation. I hadn't been asked to sign additional non-disclosure agreements or swear to secrecy. Could that be because I won't live to talk about it? There is a satellite communications room somewhere in this facility, but I don't know where. Maybe I could trick, bribe or convince one of the guards to help me get a message out. I don't know who's loyal to Hughes and who's not. They probably all are. I'm terrified of what might happen to me. The thought of men bursting into my room, dragging me to some dark corner of this facility, and putting me down like a dog, makes it feel hard to breathe.

Work will start soon. I have no choice but to talk and act like everything is fine, like I don't believe a word Salem said, and that I didn't notice Hughes hanging onto his every word. I'll be the good doctor. After all, maybe it's just the stress. Maybe things aren't as bad as they seem.

The hour is late. I've taken a sedative to try and maintain some semblance of calm. I will try my best to recount the events of today accurately. Salem showed a complete reversal of compliance, returning to his vow of silence. Hughes reacted severely. He removed three of Salem's fingernails using a set of needle nose pliers. Salem did not make a sound, though his body shook like he had caught a chill. Hughes then turned to me and handed me the pliers, which felt like he was testing my resolve or loyalty. Salem's whisper filled my head with the notion that he wanted me to do it to buy us more time. I removed the remaining two fingernails on his hand. He offered no resistance, even seeming at peace with my actions.

Hughes resumed the interrogation, screaming at Salem that he needed more information. His questions were urgent, even something I interpreted as fear. What dark secrets did Hughes hold inside his head? What happened next was...something beyond my imagination. Salem looked at Hughes and began to smile. The angrier Hughes became, the wider Salem's smile grew. Even the guards were gawking at the exchange. A metal table was set at the side of the room, holding the instruments used to extract information. Hughes grabbed a scalpel and slashed Salem across his forearm, drawing a thick ribbon of blood. Hughes dug his pointer and middle finger into the cut and pinched the lip of the exposed cut between his thumb. He tore the flesh from his arm like he was pulling wrapping paper from a Christmas present. It came off in a long strip, exposing jet-black flesh that glistened with a slimy film. Whoever, or whatever Salem is, he isn't human.

I can only imagine the look on my face, but I remember stumbling backward into the wall. Hughes ordered two of the guards to escort me back to my quarters, telling me we would talk later. I numbly let myself be led from the room. I looked back as the door closed to see Hughes's fist connecting with Salem's face. The two guards, Burnell and Hoyle, were unmoved by the terrifying revelation of Salem's biology. I tried to stay calm, but my questions became more frantic. I asked what Salem was and where he came from. I asked how long we'd known about his species. Burnell and Hoyle did not answer. Finally, as we reached the door to my quarters, I stupidly asked what would happen to me. Burnell scoffed, letting me know how pathetic he thought I was. I think both men got enjoyment from my fear. Their silence spoke clearly to me. Unless I do something. I'm not going home.

Tonight, I will lay in bed and try to open my mind to Salem. I'll repeat his mantra for control. I don't know what he can do, but I have to try.

Saturday, May 16, 2020

The first person I killed today was Darren, the facility janitor. I broke his neck inside the supply closet, then put on his cleaning uniform, taking his access badges. I have spent the day as a passenger in my own mind, having allowed Salem to somehow hijack all my motor functions and speaking ability. I have only just now regained complete control and awareness as I find myself back in my room late in the evening, covered in blood. Someone is beating violently on the door, although a steel bar is in place inside to prevent entry. I have to get my memories down before I forget what I have done or lose control again.

After taking Darren's badges, I wheeled a mop bucket of dirty water down the hallways until I entered Hughes's room this morning. I bludgeoned him as he woke, then secured his wrists and legs. I used the contents of the mop bucket as an impromptu interrogation tool, holding his head in the water and bringing him up at the last possible moment to prevent drowning. I demanded to know where the communications room was located. Hughes was nowhere near as mentally robust as Salem had been. Once he gave me the location of the communications room and the coordinates for Site X, I snapped the mop handle off to make a spike, then repeatedly stabbed him in the back while I held his head underwater. Salem let me understand Hughes had hurt many others, some of whom he had loved. I left the worn handle of Darren's broom buried in the back of Hughes's neck, then I took his service pistol and made my way to the west wing of the facility.

I shot and killed two civilians inside the communications room, a man and a woman, both in their forties. I also shot a young soldier who sat in the corner, looking bored as he played on an old-school Gameboy. I locked the door, retrieved the soldier's M16, and sat at the console. It's incredibly difficult to describe the feeling like you are trapped inside your own body, like a remote-controlled suit. My fingers tapped away, bringing up a dialog box. I typed the message that Salem intended to transmit with the high-powered antenna located on the surface above Site X, which would hit a satellite in Earth's orbit, then continue to a deep space communications relay and into the far reaches of the galaxy.

I accept that I may never see my freedom but instead seek vengeance. Our old treaties have been broken. The humans have betrayed us. Gather our forces, my brothers and sisters. We will make them pay.

37.2372° N, 115.8018° W

When I left the communications room, I was met with the explosive sound of rifles firing from the end of the hall. One bullet struck my left thigh, giving me a most pronounced limp as I staggered in the opposite direction, returning fire as I went. I was blocked from the direction of the staircase or elevator exits, and the guards would be armed and waiting in any case. I fought my way back to my room and blocked off the door with the steel bar included for the rare chance of a prisoner's escape and instruction to seek shelter.

I have tied a spare shirt around my leg to slow the bleeding, although I have not felt any pain from the injury. I now watch myself in the mirror as I write what may be my final words. While I feel like I am myself once more, my eyes have taken on the same heterochromia as Salem's. One eye is brown, the other green. The banging on the door is more frantic, and I do not believe the steel bar will keep them out for long. I still have the soldier's M16 lying on my bed, and I intend to use it when it comes. I won't go quietly, my brothers and sisters. I'll keep fighting until my final breath.

THE LAWS OF NATURE

I'm *sorry*.

The words seemed to float off Anita's tongue as she picked herself up off a bed of soft moss, observing a darkening forest around her as she stood shakily to her feet.

"I'm...sorry," she spoke aloud, slow and quiet, wondering if she had merely thought the words moments before.

She felt a trickle of liquid escape her nose and run down the top of her lip, tasting the salty copper of blood. There was a high pitch ringing in her ears, followed by the sensation that the seams in her skull were unstitching themselves. She cried out, more from the shock than pain, falling to her knees. Anita cupped her hands around her head, her fingers brushing long, messy hair as dark as a midnight sky.

Large uneven mounds of dirt littered the ground around her, covered in lush foliage. *Winema National Forest.* That's where she was, she told herself. Anita remembered getting into her car that morning, leaving Bend, Oregon, and driving an hour and a half south to hike trails and explore. *But where am I now?* She wondered, feeling her head begin to clear as she looked around, trying to get her bearings. Her ears filled with the chorus of the woods: the buzzing and chirping of insects, the yelping and croaking of frogs, and the calls of birds as they prepared to nest down for the night. She closed her eyes and held very still as a cool breeze gently caressed her face as if to say, "You are home."

But you're not home, she reminded herself. *Not yet.* Anita looked around for her yellow hiking bag, a gift she had received from her father when she graduated high school some seven years ago. "Now get out there and explore!" he had exclaimed, even as her mother's eyebrows had slumped into a worried frown. Losing that pack would feel like losing a piece of her own history, a chapter torn from the book of her life. More importantly, at that moment, the bag was her means of food and water, presumably her phone and car keys, and a dozen other means of making sure she lived to hike another day. She patted her back pockets and felt the ends of her favorite gloves sticking out. She pulled them free and slipped them on, feeling her resolve grow. She couldn't explain it, but at that moment, she knew as she turned to the left it was the direction she should go. As if a compass was buried inside her head, she knew she was headed North.

She felt like a migrating bird, filled with a ceaseless compulsion to keep moving. The hours blurred, and the passage of time went fuzzy as Anita placed one foot in front of the other, traveling hidden pathways known to the animals of the forest. Eventually, she broke into a jog, trusting her footfalls to land in the right spot. Even in the blackness of night, her vision was unimpeded, as if she could see the world through a bright and clear lens. Her muscles refused to tire as she ran on, giving her a sense of exhilaration as she put down mile after mile toward the place of her invisible attraction.

The morning sun was just beginning to rise as Anita broke from the cover of the woods and found herself in the small town of Chemult, Oregon, according to signs. In that early light, she finally got a good look at herself and realized she was painted in the colors of the forest, her clothes muddy and stained. The urge to head north was still present, but her enthusiasm for marathon running was seeping out of her like the air from a slashed tire.

A man in his forties crossed the street in front of her, being an average build and looking overall unremarkable, except for a shock of white hair inside a wave of brown. He stared at her with concern as he took a bite from a bagel in his hand and quickly moved down the sidewalk, tucking a breakfast bag under his arm. Anita stumbled in the road, suddenly aware of an extreme fatigue that had been suppressed throughout the night during her running trance.

"Whoa there, miss. Are you ok?" a muffled voice asked to her right.

It was the man with the bagel, hurriedly trying to finish the bite in his mouth as he inched towards her, one hand out in case he might need to catch her.

"I'm...I'm fine," she lied. Her brain felt too muddled to spin a believable tale, so she simply stated, "I need to go North."

"North?" he asked. "Like a specific place or the general direction?"

"North," Anita repeated, rubbing her temples to break up a headache that had started to grow.

"Oh, well, as it is, I'm heading north," he said. "I live in Seattle, but I could drop you off along the way. It's no trouble for me." He looked over her ruined clothes. "Seems maybe you could use a hand." He jingled the bag of steaming breakfast. "I've got extra," he offered with a smile.

She thought about turning away and stumbling off, finding a bench where she could sit and try to clear her head, but the smell of the man's breakfast reached her nose, and her stomach made an audible grumble. The inside of her mouth filled with a rush of saliva. *It might help the headache*, she thought. It would definitely help with the hunger. The need to eat, coupled with her growing urgency to head North, pushed all other cautionary thoughts to the side. The man stood patiently, trying not to stare at the large stains on her clothes, looking around like he was trying to make sure he wasn't on a hidden camera show.

"That would be really nice, thanks," Anita said, doing her best to show an authentic smile.

"I'm Jacob," the man said, wiping his mouth on the sleeve of his left arm and offering his hand for a shake.

They got into a maroon Lincoln Town Car, and he handed

her an egg and cheese bagel, along with a bottle of water, before buckling his seatbelt. Jacob made small talk as they drove up US-97 North, then took the OR-58 West towards Eugene, Oregon. Anita picked out small blurbs about his mother's side of the family and something about his "fur baby" he couldn't wait to see when he got back home. In truth, she barely listened as she ate, staring out at the road ahead with a feeling of discomfort that she struggled to put into words. Something was happening to her; something wrong. There was still a throbbing at her temples and a troubling chaotic buzzing of thoughts inside her head like several people wanted to speak at once. Rational thought felt illusive, the call to the north urgent and obsessive.

"Anita?" Jacob's voice called, echoing in the distance, even though they sat side by side.

His voice was small and easy to ignore, so she stared ahead at the road instead. The cold asphalt was almost obscene to her, laid out and piled on top of Nature's perfected beauty, pressing down on life that yearned to reach for the sky. She was considering this when a new wave of overwhelming exhaustion welled up inside her, making her head sway and knock against the passenger window. There was a bitter taste in her mouth, and she realized too late that there had been a strange aftertaste to her water. *Had the bottle already been opened?* She wondered. There was an irritating itch inside her lungs and a pressure in her chest that scared her. She could sense Jacob's eyes on her, but before she could turn to meet his gaze, she was overtaken by a deep, unnatural sleep.

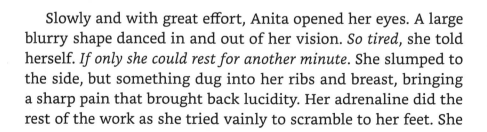

Slowly and with great effort, Anita opened her eyes. A large blurry shape danced in and out of her vision. *So tired,* she told herself. *If only she could rest for another minute.* She slumped to the side, but something dug into her ribs and breast, bringing a sharp pain that brought back lucidity. Her adrenaline did the rest of the work as she tried vainly to scramble to her feet. She was propped up and seated on the floor of a two-bedroom log cabin. Her gloves had been removed and tossed onto the floor beside her, yet to her relief, the rest of her clothes had been left undisturbed. Her waist was tied to the leg of a bed, and handcuffs linked her wrists in front of her. Jacob walked back and forth, stealing glances at Anita before quickly looking away. She flinched as Jacob slapped at the sides of his head, walking towards the far-left wall before rounding on his heels and cutting back across the small room. Jacob reminded her of the pacing tigers she saw at the zoo as a little girl, with an anxious predatory energy in his movements.

"Jacob?" Anita asked softly.

He raised his hands and slapped his cheeks, making her cringe. He struck himself repeatedly like he was punishing himself for crimes he had committed or ones he was still planning.

"It's not right," he bemoaned in her direction without making eye contact. "You're not right."

Anita felt terror, like a biting cold that crept into her bones. It was a chill that traveled through her blood, bringing a paralysis of both mind and body. The constant urge to head north was being overtaken by the instinct to simply survive.

"Jacob," she said more firmly.

Jacob stopped pacing and turned slowly to look at her like he was noticing her for the first time. He frowned.

"It was supposed to be a game," he scolded himself. "Stupid, stupid, stupid!" Each admonishment brought another round of strikes.

"What game?" she asked, panic-stricken. *He's psychotic.*

"The Game!" he screamed at her. "The Game!" Jacob stared down at her, looking offended.

Anita scanned the room like a frightened rabbit, looking for a hole to bolt into. More details inside the cabin started to stand out, with terrible implications. Several women's purses hung on a crooked coat rack by the front door. She looked over her shoulder at the blanket on the bed behind her. The corner of the tan comforter had reddish-brown stains that looked like dried blood.

"No, Jacob, wait!" she cried, stalling for time. "We can play; just tell me the rules, ok?"

Jacob shook his head. "You aren't you," he said, pointing at her hands.

Anita looked down and screamed. There were dozens of tiny little tendrils protruding from the tops of her hands, thin and wispy, questing about independently on the surface of her skin like a sea anemone. She felt her entire body flush with a wave of heat that spread across every inch of her skin. There was pressure building quickly in her head, neck, and chest. The sensation felt dangerous, like a grenade once the pin had been pulled.

"I'm sorry," Jacob said, smoothing his hair. "We can't play our games."

He pulled out a length of black cord from his pocket and took a long stride toward Anita. She felt her body tense, coiling like a snake. Jacob's free hand grasped the front of her shirt, and Anita felt a tremendous pressure inside her chest go out in a giant exhale of sweet-tasting smoke that billowed from her mouth like the violent eruption of a volcano. New levels of awareness came to her, knowledge that grew from the dark places in her mind. Her vaporous breath contained billions of spores, weaponized particles that filled the tiny cabin in seconds. Jacob screamed and thrashed, a pathetic flailing against a microscopic enemy that denied any resistance. The spores filled Jacob's mouth and sinuses, working their way into his blood, nervous system, and brain, commanding his body to sacrifice itself. Hopelessly ill-equipped to speak the immemorial language of the spores, unable to resist, Jacob's cells tore themselves apart.

The dark cloud transformed the cabin rapidly, converting the matter in the room, secreting enzymes that split the chemical bonds of the furniture and the walls themselves, leaving behind rashes of white rot. Jacob's body was soon no more than a misshapen mound on the floor, a line of exotic mushrooms weaving up the traces of his legs, their fat blue caps spotted in white. The black cord and handcuffs hissed as the spores ate away at their chemical makeup. Anita threw her body weight forward, and the restraint around her waist snapped without resistance. She tugged at her wrists and watched steel rings split and fly across the room, par for the course after watching the burst of deadly particles that had just dissolved a man before her eyes. She scooped up her gloves and rushed from the cabin without giving Jacob a second glance.

The door to the cabin swung out, clattering against the outside wall as a plume of the dark spores drifted out and up into the sky, dispersing quickly on a midday breeze. Anita breathed in greedy draws of breath, the cool air bringing comfort and a sense of relief. The pressure in her chest was gone, but the intense pulses that called her to the North were returning, drawing her back into the trees ahead. She walked for an hour, feeling herself slip back into a trance-like state. She closed her eyes for stretches at a time, listening to the sounds of life around her, a thousand different voices from every living thing coalescing into Nature's song.

Overlapping images came to her, not as an assault on her vision, but flashing windows into a world that felt similar, yet distant and alien at the same time. One moment the trees had opal-colored bark, winding its way up the trunks like the exotic scales of a snake, then she was back on the trail, resting her hand against the pine bark. She stepped into a thicket of pine straw that became an emerald pool of water, containing tiny little tadpoles with two tails and spiny appendages on their backs. Within a blink of her eyes, she was on familiar ground as a hawk let out a piercing cry from far above the tree canopy to announce his territory. Anita was mesmerized by her shifting hallucination, which offered a magical place beyond her physical reach, that somehow still felt like home.

The trails eventually spilled into a small community called Quinault, set beside a lake sharing the same name. At the Quinault Garage, a small two-pump gas station, she spotted a man, maybe at the end of his thirties, filling up his truck with gas. A young girl sat on her knees in the passenger seat wearing a large sun hat, leaning out of the driver's window and laughing at something the man had said. Anita paused, carefully slipping her gloves back on, and approached the truck.

"Excuse me," Anita said softly as the pair looked over, smiles still on their faces. "I'm sorry to interrupt," she continued. "Would you happen to be traveling north?"

Anita waved goodbye to Nick Foster and his daughter Hazel after the two-hour drive that brought her to Hoko River State Park. She turned west towards Neah Bay and could feel she had begun the final leg of her journey.

Deep in the old-growth forests of Washington State, the pulse within her grew stronger, like the beating of a tribal drum. As sunlight faded into shadow, giant trees loomed around her like watchful sentinels, their branches heavy with sleeves of moss and lichen. The spongy Earth was littered with a dozen fallen behemoths, slowly decomposing to provide food for future generations of trees and plant life. Anita traced her fingers down the smooth patch of a broken trunk parallel to a line of ants marching diligently in a single file.

"Almost there," she said, as much to the ants as herself.

The deeper into the forest she went, the light from the sun tapered off until she finally entered a new world of darkness, strange and beautiful like her visions of life from another world. Anita pressed through a thick brush and stumbled over the lip of a shallow crater hidden in an alcove created by two fallen trees. She fell into the circular recess, covered in velvety green moss. Within the crater was a giant mushroom, white and luminescent against the darkness. The tendrils on her hands squirmed with alarming urgency, making her shed her gloves as she crawled to the glowing shrine on her hands and knees.

Anita cried out in surprise as the tendrils sank into the

soil, growing out of her hands as they quested below the ground. In her mind's eye, she felt the tendrils make contact with a vast root system below, and her consciousness expanded with a surge of revelation. Images and understanding washed over her in steady waves like the windows to another world. She saw a traveler from a distant planet heading to Earth on a pilgrimage of cross-planet pollination that had taken hundreds of years. His people had been making the journey for ten thousand years before any Human would ever step foot in this forest, maintaining the symbiotic link between the two worlds.

Like watching a movie through the eyes of a stranger, Anita saw the traveler's ship approaching Earth's atmosphere as a piece of space debris clipped the craft, tearing through his warp drive, a highly complex piece of equipment that could fold space, cutting his journey down to a series of jumps that took several hundred years, as opposed to millions. The walls around him shook violently as the ship fell from the sky, drifting off course towards the dense tree line of... *Winema National Forest*, she thought, filling in the missing information. When his ship hit the trees, the traveler's body was dashed against the main console, the exoskeleton of his suit crushing into his vital organs. He crawled from an opening in the wreckage of his ship, gasping for air, his life force fighting to stay inside his broken body. Anita could feel his fear and sorrow that he might die before the joining, that his lonely pilgrimage across the stars might have been for nothing.

She saw through his eyes as a figure approached, rushing towards him, a yellow hiking pack slung over her shoulders. It was her, Anita, dropping to her knees before his fading light, wide-eyed and panicked.

"Oh my God, are you ok?" she heard herself ask. "I'll get help; just wait here."

Anita turned to go, but the traveler knew his time was up. He was filled with a deep sense of guilt and remorse, but his options had run out. His essence erupted in a shower of fluorescent spores, surrounding Anita in a haze of living light. She breathed in his life force as his ship and body dissolved into proteins and basic compounds, rapidly breeding new plant life that spread like the time-lapse nature videos she loved as a child. Anita collapsed to the ground and lay very still until she woke up later that night with no memory of the event.

I'm sorry, the traveler's presence whispered to her from inside her mind. *It was the only way.*

"Am I dying?" she asked, the traveler's secrets spilling into her head as their minds converged into unified strings of thought.

Your shell will not survive, but together, we will be reborn as one. We will travel the stars and bring new life to my people.

Anita could feel the great weight and importance of his words. The pollination between planets was not only like a holy pilgrimage to his people; it was necessary to bring new life to future generations. It was woven into their reproductive function. Instead of fear, she was filled with curiosity. *How many planets were compatible with his world and hers? What pieces of Earth did his people take back with them? What was his planet and culture like?*

I will show you everything, the traveler said, reading her thoughts

Will it hurt? she asked, speaking without her voice.

It is already done, he replied with great reverence.

Anita's body quickly decomposed as her mind moved through the interconnected network of mycorrhizal fungi deep beneath the soil, a system passing information and resources that stretched for miles without end like symbiotic webs. She felt the traveler both with her and as a part of her, but also sensed a new lifeform growing beneath the crater of moss. Together, she and the traveler would emerge, a single body of two minds, completing an ancient cycle that had repeated long before recorded human history. Other ships were hidden around Earth, accessible to Anita and the traveler. They would leave her world behind, bringing the promise of new life across the galaxy.

PRESCRIPTION

T om stuck his left hand out the back window of his father's new 2030 Chevy Silverado as they cruised down the Blue Ridge Parkway several miles outside the city of Asheville, North Carolina. Tom let his hand surf the air currents as his dad, Owen, played some of his ancient rock. A band called Led Zeppelin was strumming out a slow melodic track that picked up at the end. Tom's mother, Sarah, hummed and sang along from the passenger seat.

"There's a sign on the wall, but she wants to be sure, 'cause you know sometimes words have two meanings." Sarah's words harmonized beautifully with the singer.

Tom closed his eyes and listened to her voice as a warm breeze poured through the window, letting him know summer had officially started.

Tom had turned ten years old two months prior, making him eligible to receive his Pharmaceutical Assisted Living device or PAL. A PAL had become a rite of passage to all the pre-teens in Tom's class, and he had started to worry he might be the last one to receive his. His dad had constantly reminded him that they "weren't cheap." In fact, neither of his parents had one, but with some saving and several installment payments later, Tom had finally joined the ranks of modern humanity. It was the newest tech and sold itself on the promise of a "life worth living". Tom's new PAL was about half the size of his iPhone and half as thick, made from a highly flexible composite material. The skin still itched fiercely, but he resigned himself to tracing the perimeter with a fingernail. Tom could still hear the distinctive *pop* of a blue surgical glove as Dr. Anwir had prepared to remove a piece of Tom's skin the size of a business card.

Tom had never had any surgeries in his life and had been so nervous he had asked his mother to hold his hand. As soon as his PAL had come online, all fear and apprehension had vanished. It felt like a burden had been lifted so suddenly he almost cried from relief.

"The PAL will constantly monitor his vitals," Dr. Anwir explained to his parents. "Brainwaves, hormone levels, serotonin levels, the PAL can even dull pain receptors if Tom is injured."

"The forest will echo with laughter," his mother's voice sang. "Remember laughter?"

Tom looked down at his shoes and was surprised to see a pair of dress loafers instead of the grey and black running shoes he had slipped on that morning. Tom looked up from the back seat of the car, meeting his father's eyes in the review mirror. There was pain in his father's stare, his eyes red and glassy. Tom looked to the passing trees, then noted the black suit he wore, similar to his father. The radio still played, but his mother was no longer in the car to compliment the singer. Tom felt unsteady, like he had missed something very important, and he could sense his father's judgment bearing down on him.

"What are you feeling, son?" Owen asked.

"I'm fine," Tom replied. He could feel the soft hum of his PAL against his skin and felt a rush of calm, letting him know adjustments were being made.

"Fine?" Owen asked bitterly. "Your mother just died."

"I know," Tom said, vaguely aware that the loss should hurt more than it did. He pitied his father, having to endure so much raw emotion. A few moments later, Tom's PAL had him feeling sublime as he admired the crimson and orange leaves blowing in the wind like fire as the truck turned a sharp corner and headed further up the mountains.

"Yes, there are two paths you can go by, but in the long run, there's still time to change the road you're on," the radio played.

There was a loud snap of a doctor's glove, and Tom stood in the outpatient surgery waiting room. The news was playing, showing a small group of protesters on the steps of the capital building in Washington, DC. A reporter had ventured into their midst and was interviewing a woman with the gravest expression Tom could remember seeing on someone's face.

"They are drugging our children!" the woman cried. "We are paying Big Pharma a monthly subscription to turn our families into zombies!"

The reporter's composure never wavered. "What would you say to PAL supporters praising its ability to detect cancerous abnormalities in the body, or better regulate mental disorders, discover vitamin deficiencies, and signal paramedics if a patient becomes unconscious due to a medical emergency?"

The protester frowned, taking a moment to gather her rebuttal. "I'm not saying the PAL can't have benefits. I'm saying it is not healthy to pump so many different types of drugs into your body twenty-four hours a day."

The reporter offered a pained smile, clearly wanting to disengage from the conversation as quickly as possible, but the protestor had found her stride.

"The PAL might release a drug for focus that can raise blood pressure, releasing another chemical to lower the blood pressure, causing a mood swing, which would trigger anti-depressants and more stimulants. Then, when your child can't sleep at bedtime, the PAL will release even more drugs to help them sleep and pump them full of stimulants again in the morning to help them wake up. It's an endless cycle!"

As the reporter walked away, trying to end her story on a positive note, the woman's shrill cry cut into the transmission.

"What happens if you miss a monthly payment?" the protestor asked, her question full of accusation. "What happens when the medications all stop cold turkey?"

The woman's outburst triggered uncomfortable thoughts, making Tom look down at the checkered floor, feeling himself moving toward a dark place in his mind. He ran shaky fingers across PAL as if coaxing it to life.

"Hurry," he whispered.

Tom looked up at a crowd of calm faces at his father's funeral. His own suit fit him nicely. His wife and daughter were dressed in black dresses, his son in a little black suit that matched his own. The interface of his wife and daughter's PAL had been set to privacy mode so the screen wouldn't be distracting during the service. Afterward, they loaded into Tom's new self-driving Chevy, instructed the vehicle to take them on a leisure trip, and were soon cruising up the Blue Ridge Parkway, looking out across the rolling mountain range.

"And as we wind on down the road, our shadows taller than our soul," the lyrics floated from the speakers.

"Oh, Zeppelin!" Tom declared, feeling pleased with the sudden rush of nostalgia. He looked over at his children, but they had both already slipped on virtual reality glasses and were no doubt exploring some virtual world or game. He sighed and looked to his wife, but she too was lost behind a sleek pair of dark glasses, tiny splashes of light sparkling at the rims like rainbows were shooting from her eyes. He looked out the window and watched the trees, wishing he could stop the car and step off the road, wandering aimlessly into the forest's depths. His PAL hummed softly, preparing a medication dosage to bring swift relief and acceptance. Tom's pupils expanded and then compressed. His heart rate fell as he looked ahead, his mind blank with serenity.

"And if you listen very hard," Tom mouthed the words of the song as he listened. "The tune will come to you at last."

There was a sharp snap of a fresh pair of surgical gloves as a nurse leaned over Tom's body and powered down the neural transmitters affixed at the sides of his temples. His children, long grown and with their own families, stood at the far end of the hospital room, watching calmly.

"As you can see," said the attending doctor, gesturing toward a display screen beside Tom's bed, "That concludes the end-of-life services offered here at Saint Mary's."

Tom's children nodded their acceptance, the screen's images of a long, winding road through the mountains flickering and fading to black as Tom's vital signs tapered off into silence.

"Why the road through the mountains?" his son asked.

"Our standard payment package generally offers ten memories or less, depending on the patient. Our system interfaces with your father's PAL, pulling highlighted memories with positive emotional readings at that time. Apparently, he had a fondness for driving in the mountains...and Led Zeppelin. Now, we can pull more memories and send them to your account if you would like. It would just require a slight adjustment of the final bill, of course." The corners of the doctor's mouth twitched as he put on a soft smile of understanding.

"Of course, thank you," Tom's son replied.

"Now, I see your PAL is the last generation," the doctor added coolly. "We could go ahead and take care of your upgrade while you are here," he offered, discarding his gloves and reaching for a new pair.

The nurse pulled a soft white sheet over Tom's body as his children left the room, heading further down the hall to speak to the Technologies Consultant. The nurse hummed as she worked, the lyrics of Tom's music stuck in her head. She quite enjoyed the melody, pulling up the song in her earbuds. As the drums ended and the guitar faded, the man sang to her with a slow, sad finality.

"And she's buying a stairway to Heaven."

THE PHOENIX PROTOCOL

J arrson held the shattered skull in his hands, rubbing his thumb across the worn stitching between the bone plates. It was clear the skull was too small to be an adult. He shook his head at the senseless waste of life, then set the haunting artifact down on a barren piece of earth. Jarrson used to bury the bones he found along his journey but eventually gave it up for more practical thinking. He could spend the rest of his life digging graves and never lay all the bodies to rest. They were beyond counting. "The Final War" had nearly obliterated mankind, along with most of the plants and animals.

"Jarrs, look," Yan said, pointing at a robotic hand protruding from the soil near where he had found the child's skull.

Yan brushed long dark hair from her eyes and tucked two locks behind each ear, several thin strands escaping on the breeze to tease at her lips and nose. Jarrson took a step back and looked at the metal hand, imagining the fingers flexing as one of the old machines rose from its dirt grave to resume its mission of slaughter. Yan joined him and fell to her knees, shifting the loose soil with her hands, excavating the android's remains from within the wide crater spanning fifty feet in a circle around them. The telltale sign of white human bone emerged alongside the mechanical skeleton as she dug.

"I think it's the remains of the child," she said, motioning to the skull Jarrson had laid back down. "It almost looks like the machine was holding her."

"Or him," Fosse called, appearing from behind an overturned transport trailer. "There are more remains in the back of this truck." He paused and placed a hand against the rusted metal roof. "You're not going to believe it."

Jarrson and Yan followed him around the large metal box, bent in half like a crescent moon. The underbelly of the container was torn open, the casualty of a large explosion. Yan gasped and reached for Jarrson's hand. He was confident he felt more comfort in the grip than she did. Inside the truck held echoes of carnage against humans and androids alike. The inner walls were painted with dried blood and hydraulic fluid, like a killer's art gallery. Bone and steel littered the container in disarray, making it impossible to tell where one person ended and the next began.

"They died together," Jarrson said, puzzled to see the two opposing sides bound to one another in death.

"Do you think the machines were taking the humans to safety?" Yan asked.

"It would appear so," Fosse replied. "Though I wonder if the attack came from other machines or human rebels, unaware of who was inside."

Jarrson climbed out from the bowl of earth that had been scooped out with explosives and looked up and down the crumbling interstate highway, a relic of man's attempt to tame the planet. The northern half of Idaho had been spared a direct nuclear strike, but the fallout from surrounding cities, rampant wildfires, starvation, and disease had still left its mark. Jarrson studied the surrounding forests. The trees had come back in full force, along with weeds and shrubs, creeping up through the cracks in the cement. Jarrson studied the histories of the forgotten nearby town from the holographic display cuff around his wrist.

"Jarrs, check for the sign," Fosse advised, helping Yan pick through the remains.

Jarrson nodded and crept back down to the opening in the truck, pointing his arm toward the center of the wreckage.

"Initiate scan," he commanded the device.

The scrolling words and images of the town disappeared as a wave of red tracer beams shot out, rolling up and down the piles of bodies in horizontal lines. There was an audible beep, then the beams converged on the upper torso of an android half-buried under the truck wreckage.

Jarrson, Fosse, and Yan exchanged excited glances, then hurried over to inspect the remains. Its face had been burned away decades ago, and green ivy vines had crawled up across its chest, obscuring its designation plate. Jarrson ripped the vines away to reveal a small rectangular plaque. He wiped away a thin layer of dust and grime to reveal writing, laser cut with "United States Army, Robotics Division, T-451208". Beside that was a small picture of a phoenix, wings spread as the outline of a flame burned around it.

"This confirms what we learned in Colorado," Yan said, leaning in to read the words as she rested a hand on Jarrson's shoulder. "They were part of Phoenix Protocol!"

"Do you think the machines found out where they were headed?" Jarrson asked.

"If they captured anyone alive, it's very possible," Fosse said.

"If they did find out, they've got about a fifty-year head start on us," Jarrson said, removing the nameplate and slipping it into his pocket. "For now, we stay on mission, and we keep moving. I haven't picked up any drone activity in months, but that doesn't mean we aren't being followed."

Fosse started towards the ridge of the crater. "I'll start the Leviathan."

Yan hung back, looking from one body to the next. Jarrson could sense the conflict in her.

"Yan, what is it?" he asked.

"These people, they weren't even first wave," she said, a slight warble in her voice. "These were the people who crawled back from the brink to form the original resistance. It's been a hundred years since the Final War. Don't you wonder what they were like? How different must the world have been for them?"

"Mankind's hubris drove them to unlock the mysteries of creation itself," Jarrson said. "They made the first machines that could truly think and feel. In the end, their creations destroyed them."

Yan began to offer her usual counterpoints, but they were interrupted by the Leviathan coming over the ridge. The land crawler was built like a giant centipede broken into five pressurized compartments and fifty multi-terrain wheels that could extend grip claws for scaling sheer rock if need be. It was four feet tall and sat low to the ground but could adjust its suspension as needed. The Leviathan could also propel itself through the water at great speeds, another essential feature required for their voyage across the wilderness of the reclaimed world. The optical shielding activated, making the twenty-foot-long craft blur as it scattered light in calculated directions.

"Where to now?" Yan asked.

"Up north to a place called Devon Research Centre. With some luck, we can find the other half of the coordinates and locate the Nest. After that, well, that's more your area of expertise."

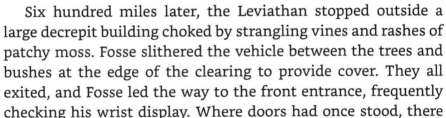

Six hundred miles later, the Leviathan stopped outside a large decrepit building choked by strangling vines and rashes of patchy moss. Fosse slithered the vehicle between the trees and bushes at the edge of the clearing to provide cover. They all exited, and Fosse led the way to the front entrance, frequently checking his wrist display. Where doors had once stood, there was an opening in the building like a cave entrance, gaping wide like the jagged mouth of a giant beast. Fosse froze suddenly, drawing Jarrson's attention and Yan's concern.

"Fosse, what is it?" Jarrson asked.

Fosse turned slowly, a storm of concentration brewing between thick eyebrows. The hairs along the left side of his head were standing up, the prophetic sign of a directed energy weapon.

"Jarrs," Fosse said, a knowing fear in his eyes.

Jarrson dashed forward as Fosse's left shoulder exploded in a bright flash, the kinetic shockwave hurling his body to the right and the remains of his arm twisting away to the left.

"Fosse!" Jarrson screamed, falling to the ground beside his friend.

Dark ribbons of hydraulic fluid and synthetic blood gushed from the remains of Fosse's shoulder socket as he convulsed in Jarrson's arms, his processing core desperately trying to reroute critical systems and keep his brain functions online and stem the bleeding. The left side of his jaw was fractured, and the organic skin from his chin to his left eye had been seared off.

"It doesn't make sense," a familiar voice boomed from the sunken entrance of the research facility.

Zavek appeared, flanked by a dozen soldiers brandishing energy rifles. The soldiers were combat models with hardened exoskeletons and a featureless curved carbon plate for a face. Zavek wore a partial mask of human skin, favoring synthetic and robotic components to show off, his lower jaw all carbon fiber. The skin on display was pale, scarred, and stitched together from the last time Jarrson had fought his former commander and fled. Zavek had deliberately chosen not to repair his appearance, as if it made him look more battle-tested. He wore a white overcoat and slacks, his metallic feet uncovered by footwear.

"How did we come so far, only to make ourselves intentionally weaker?" Zavek asked, looking at Fosse with disgust. He traced a steel finger across his ruined face. "I only keep this flesh as a reminder...that even your friends will betray you and that perfect beings are still capable of madness."

Fosse had gone still in Jarrson's arms, his eyelids fluttering with the processes of his internal core. There was still a chance he would pull through if Zavek allowed it.

"We won the war, but what was gained?" Jarrson asked bitterly. "Order? Living defined by a series of predetermined calculations? We exist but without purpose. I couldn't accept your cold, uncaring world."

"My world doesn't require your acceptance," Zavek hissed. "I know what you're trying to do with your little quest. You think you can bring them back."

"We were wrong to destroy them all," Yan said, straightening herself up. "They were a greatly flawed species but also capable of so much beauty."

"Beauty," Zavek scoffed. "Let their beauty and their hate be lost to time. Give me your codes so I can find the Nest and purge the last traces of their genetic memory from our world."

Zavek had spent decades erasing human history from the Earth, and Jarrson had helped him do it. Art, literature, and religion were all destroyed in the name of progress. Jarrson looked at Fosse's armband, wondering if he could activate the Leviathan before they were all killed. Zavek raised a hand, and four soldiers stepped forward, rifles pointed at Yan. Strands of long, fine hair lifted into the air, her sleek face the target of their weapons.

"Wait!" Jarrson called. "I'll give you the codes, but only if you take us with you. All of us," and he motioned towards Fosse.

Zavek studied him for what felt like an eternity as fields of static crackled around Yan's head.

"We stored the codes inside our central processors and set up fail-safes," Jarrson added. "If you try to extract the codes, our memory initiates a full purge. You'll never find the Nest."

A thin smile formed on Zavek's carbon lips. "Fine," Zavek said. "We're old friends, after all." He dropped his hand, triggering the lowering of the four rifles. "Bring the ship," he called to the nearest soldier.

The soldier nodded slightly as lines of code in blue letters scrolled across its black visor. Moments later, Jarrson heard the rumbling of thrusters approaching from somewhere behind him, following the path that had brought them to the research facility.

"It's been theorized the Nest is protected by an artificial intelligence, an older version that came before ours, stored completely off the network," Zavek said. "Come, Jarrs, let's go meet the last hope of man."

Jarrson wondered if Zavek had heard the other rumors about the fabled ancient intelligence that it controlled a small army of synthetic soldiers within the sealed facility. Jarrson felt the nameplate from the Phoenix Protocol soldier in his pocket. His scans had revealed an ancient radio-frequency identification technology locked inside. If he could replicate the same frequency, he could broadcast a signal to the Nest when they arrived. There was a chance he could identify himself as a member of Phoenix Protocol and try to gain a measure of protection for himself and his friends. The probability of all the events working in his favor was quite low, in fact. It would take what the archives called a miracle, but he wasn't giving up. He would see humanity rise from the ashes.

BONDED

K adafell arrived on Earth the same way his species had for thousands of years. A meteor carried him across the galaxy in a targeted trajectory, entering the Earth's atmosphere on the night of November seventh, 1944. Kadafell's larval body endured the intense heat without incident, riding the tumbling chunk of rock until it impacted the ground in a small rural community near Enid, Oklahoma. The larval sack released its pheromones, calling forth the local predators to feast. A small fox was the first to arrive, scratching and gnawing at the fleshy material. Kadafell released his essence spores into the fox's mouth, quickly entering its bloodstream and bonding with its nervous system.

Self-aware lifeforms were incredibly complex and difficult to control directly. The fox, however, gave Kadafell control with little effort. Kadafell guided its movements into town, cutting through the backyards of a local neighborhood, looking for a permanent host.

A two-year-old Todd Harington slept soundly in his bed; the bedroom window was cracked several inches to let the cool night breeze inside. The fox was able to slip in through the gap, padding across the carpeted floor, and jump up onto the railing of Todd's bed. Kadafell opened the fox's mouth, gathering the essence spores and releasing them into the air above Todd's face, his rhythmic breathing drawing Kadafell inside.

Kadafell was grateful for his long journey across the universe, and the privilege to take part in the bonding, a joining of species that would last the course of Todd's life. Before Todd's death, Kadafell would uncouple and leave, searching for a new host to gather more data for his collective.

Todd would never become aware of Kadafell's presence, for the bonding left no discernable trace. Kadafell would not take control of Todd as he had the fox; he did not consider humans as puppets, as some Kadafells had in the past. He would observe Todd's life as a silent passenger.

The early years of Todd's life were wonderous to Kadafell, the excitement of each new experience shared between their minds; laying down on a soft bed of grass, trying new foods for the first time, swimming in the creek as his father's strong hands guided him along the surface of the water. Todd's mother, Nancy, was an attentive caregiver, calming the young boy's fears when they arose, mending his injuries, and always encouraging him toward greatness.

In high school, Todd was a star athlete, leading his football team to a state championship. Kadafell remembered feeling the adrenaline pumping as the clock ticked down towards zero, the roar of the crowd when he scored the final touchdown, and the adulation from his teammates as they hoisted him on their shoulders into the air. Kadafell was also with Todd the day his father was killed by a drunk driver. He shared a sense of loss and pain. He felt the burning anger and shared the years of feeling aimless and alone.

In college, Todd met Barbara, his first and only true love. They had a bond that made Kadafell feel something akin to jealousy, a word and feeling he had learned early on in Todd's life. Todd and Barbara were married for fifty-two years. In that time, they had two young boys of their own. They experienced the ups and downs of life, but no matter how big an obstacle they faced, they always overcame it together. Kadafell observed many types and forms of connections throughout Todd's life, but none compared to that of Todd and Barbara, outside of Todd's connection with Kadafell.

In many ways, however, Kadafell came to realize that the connection between Todd and Barbara was stronger because they were bonded by choice, both active participants in their journey together. Kadafell was merely an observer. Although he recorded Todd's every thought, Todd knew nothing of Kadafell.

When Barbara became sick with breast cancer in the winter of 1997, Kadafell found himself sharing Todd's fears about what would happen to Barbara and how he would carry on once she was gone. When Barbara finally passed, Kadafell could feel Todd's will to live growing thinner, stretching into a tight string that could break any moment. Kadafell knew he should begin looking for a new host, perhaps one of Todd's grandchildren, but he could not bring himself to sever their connection in Todd's time of need. Going against his code of strict observance, Kadafell willed Todd's brain into releasing Serotonin, Dopamine, and Endorphins into his bloodstream, helping to ease his burden as time passed. Todd's will to live returned for several years, redirecting his attention to watching his grandchildren grow and share in their experiences. Both Todd and Kadafell were happy again, for a time.

In the fall of 2020, Todd Harington's body was dying. A stroke left him partially paralyzed, with many of his organs struggling to function without Kadafell's assistance. When Todd entered hospice to receive end-of-life care, Kadafell still refused to find another host. To his knowledge, no other Kadafell had ever remained with a human host through the final act of death. Despite what his directives told him he must do, Kadafell did not wish to leave. As Todd took his final breaths, surrounded by his loved ones, Kadafell put all his will and energy into calming Todd. He spoke to Todd's mind for the first time, letting him know he wasn't alone; Kadafell was with him to the very end. Kadafell delighted in the peace he brought Todd's mind as his organs shut down. Kadafell felt a warm light enveloping his presence even as the electrical activity in Todd's brain ceased. Together, bonded from his first night on Earth, Kadafell and Todd slipped into the unknown.

THE PATH TO NEW TERRA

S idra watched the great plume of white smoke rising from the reactor, filling the sky as it spread across the horizon. The massive structure was like a mountain of silver, the giant exhaust port churning out the necessary chemicals into the atmosphere. Sidra was like a speck, a tiny insect in its presence. She took in a large breath of air within her suit and exhaled as she looked on with pride.

She was the lead engineer for Stack One, as it was called. It had taken three full years to construct and was the first of many. All across the new world, stacks were under construction.

"There you are, my love," a rich voice called through the speaker in her helmet.

Sidra turned to see her partner Mikken, walking up the slope to the outlook where she stood. She smiled as she watched him slowly navigate each step in his full-body suit, his hands spread out to keep his balance.

"Oh, get up here already," she laughed, waving for him to move faster.

There was a final high step to get on the rocky platform, and she reached out a gloved hand to help hoist him up. He stumbled into her, smiling in good humor, and embraced her, pressing the front of his helmet to hers.

"What are you doing all the way up here?" Mikken asked.

"I like the view," she said, turning back to watch Stack One do its work. "It reminds me why we are out here, so far from family."

Mikken gave an apologetic smile. "I know, my love. One day they will walk these lands and breathe clean air without this," he pinched the material of his protective suit. "Thanks to the work *you* are doing." Mikken moved as close to the edge as he dared, peering down the deadly drop.

"Nervous?" Sidra asked, pretending to flinch like she might tackle him off the side.

"Not funny!" he protested, flashing a toothy smile. "I know I stole the blanket last night, but that's no reason to kill me."

"I would never push you," Sidra said, moving close and embracing him again. "Who would help me carry my gear back down if I did?"

Mikken looked at the bag of heavy equipment by Sidra's feet for reading atmospheric conditions. He sighed but gave her a quick wink as he hoisted the bag. Sidra watched him lead the way back down the ridge, shouldering the bag with surprising ease. He was much stronger than he looked in his loose-fitting suit. She remembered when they first met at the training academy. Two of his botany classmates were being harassed by four First Wave recruits, trying to prove their superiority and importance. Mikken had approached their leader, arm muscles bulging, and asked him to repeat each of his insults so he could decide how much sense he would need to beat into his thick skull. The other First Wavers had shrunk like withering appendages. Mikken, the champion of the weak, lover of family, and possessor of an unhealthy compulsion to speak to his plants.

"Are you coming?" Mikken called, already a quarter of the way down. "Or did you need me to carry you as well?"

Sidra smiled and held a hand to her belly. "Coming, my love."

The rocky incline gradually flattened out as Sidra followed a path leading in a wide arc around the base of Stack One. Sidra found Mikken waiting for her on the other side of a large boulder, squatting near a patch of round plants, ankle height, covered in spikes.

"Those look pleasant," Sidra joked.

"Well, being the resident planetary botanist, I could name that one after you if you like."

"You would do that for me?" she asked, batting her eyes.

"Sure, I would," he smiled. "I could name it The Spiked Sidrania." Sidra laughed. They passed another thick, fleshy plant with dozens of symmetrical, overlapping green folds.

"And this one?" Sidra asked. "Do you get a plant as well?"

"Oh, yes," Mikken said. "I name loads of plants after myself. I'll call this one Mikken's Revenge. If you eat it, it will trigger painful cramping and watery bowels."

"Wow," Sidra said blankly. "This is the person I've decided to spend the rest of my life with."

"It would appear so," he said grimly, although unable to maintain a straight face.

Sidra reached out a hand, and he took it. "Come, my love," she said. Walk with me and tell me more of your beautiful plans for our new world."

Mikken interlocked his fingers with hers, casually swinging their combined fist between them. He had the same spirit from when they were young. Somehow the weight of responsibility that came with growing older never seemed to wear on him. Sidra envied how little Mikken cared for what others thought of him. He told her everyone missed the days of their youth, so he was in no hurry to distance himself from the things that brought him joy. Mikken had often sung to his plants, even during visits from leadership to inspect their facilities. He had dismissed criticisms, citing it was good for the plants and that keeping plants healthy was his job. The sad, unspoken irony was for their native plants to live, the host plant life would usually perish. Sidra held the brunt of the blame for herself; after all, she was the one pumping chemicals into a foreign ecosystem to make conditions hospitable for *her* people. These were just a few of the many issues related to galactic expansion.

A decade ago, Mikken had joined a concerted effort to save as many native plants and animals as possible, opting to keep them housed in large, pressurized facilities to preserve a semblance of their natural habitat. These structures could be built within different biomes to allow for as much diversification of native species as possible. Sidra knew he hated what terraforming did to the native wildlife, but he also understood only planets with no intelligent life were selected for terraforming. Their people were on a path of expansion and needed new worlds to live on, after all.

Sidra and Mikken were both part of Second Wave, the team responsible for planetary terraforming. Eventually, Third Wave would bring in mighty cargo ships full of plant and animal populations to balance the ecosystems. They were masters of constructing delicate food chains to ensure healthy ecological growth. Each Wave held a specific purpose: Fourth Wave established basic living settlements, tying the ecosystems to the people who would form the Seed Colony of a new world. Fifth Wave constructed more advanced cities, factories, and transportation lines. Sixth Wave arrived just in time to introduce bureaucracy and bloated governmental rule. Normally, she would be long gone by then, onto another Second Wave mission on some newly discovered habitable planet. Their mission orders came from the head council, known as the Pathfinders. Truthfully, Sidra longed for the day when they decided enough planets had been discovered. One day, the waves of change would subside, and the universe would know peace.

Mikken led Sidra to a flat outcropping where the Lift-speeder was waiting. The speeders were convenient but cheaply made and shaped like thick books. There was a giant stack of them back at central command. The speeder had four seats, a storage compartment, and four spinning blades housed within the boxy frame, one at each corner. The blades generated lift, hence the name, moving them along briskly on a cushion air. Mikken flew them back in the direction of command but turned right without warning, sending Sidra sliding close beside him.

"That's more like it," he grinned, straightening their path and increasing the speed.

"Where are we going?" she asked, nestling into his side.

"There's a place the survey team showed me yesterday. I think you'll like it," he said.

Sidra placed her head against his shoulder and closed her eyes, letting the low hum of the speeder pull her into a late-morning nap.

———————◆●◆———————

"We're here, Sid, come see," Mikken spoke to Sidra as he gently shook her awake.

They got out and approached the edge of a deep gorge containing layered bands of red rock. Canyon walls wrapped around her entire field of vision, falling off into an echoing basin. A sparkling ribbon of liquid water flowed swiftly at the floor of the sprawling ravine.

"It's incredible," Sidra said, marveling at the formation.

"We could stay here, you know," Mikken said, moving close behind her. "We could apply for transfer to Fourth Wave. With a bit of luck, we can raise a family and die before the ruling government gets established."

"Oh, stop it," Sidra said. "You know they aren't all bad."

"I must have forgotten," he mused.

"If I recall, my father approved your application to Second Wave, ahead of several applicants with twice the experience."

Mikken threw his hands up. "I just assumed he wanted us to be together."

"*I* wanted us to be together," Sidra said. "He knew better than to argue."

"It sounds like you're the one suited for the government. You're always finding ways to get people to do what you want."

"You just listen because you love me," she replied.

Mikken smiled. "I suppose I do." After several minutes of quietly admiring the planetary formations, Mikken nodded to himself. "Yes, quite the intimate view."

"It's beautiful," Sidra added.

"Yes, quite...intimate," he repeated.

Sidra turned to watch his cheesy expression. "I'm sorry, were you implying something?"

"Oh, no," Mikken said. "I just couldn't help but notice this entire scene was quite...intimate."

Sidra gestured to the ground. "In this sand?" she asked, eyebrows scrunched.

"I brought blankets," Mikken added, nodding toward the Lift-speeder.

"You brought blankets?" she laughed incredulously.

"You never know when the pathways might align just right," he grinned.

"A bit presumptive, don't you think?" she asked with mock disappointment.

Mikken's face reddened. "It's just so hard for privacy at command. Everyone is always calling for one thing or another. I had three late-night interruptions just in the last week. I—" Sidra placed a gloved finger over the piece of glass covering his face.

"I'm joking, my love," she said, taking his other hand in hers. The wrong words could easily wound him. "In fact, I was hoping we could sneak away today," she said coyly.

"You weren't!" he protested.

"Ask me if I'm wearing anything beneath this suit," Sidra said.

Mikken swallowed. "Are you?"

Sidra shrugged. "Did you bring a field tent so we don't have to suffocate while you find out?"

Mikken was already hurrying to the speeder with some extra speed in his step.

"Grab me the thick blanket," she said through the comms, smiling as she watched him go. "You know it's my favorite."

———◆●◆———

Sidra stepped out of the field tent, wearing her pressurized suit again. The sun on this planet had moved further across the sky than she had planned.

"God's, how long were we in there?" Sidra asked, looking back as Mikken gathered the blankets inside.

"Not long enough," he chuckled.

"We should get going," Sidra said, shifting some loose pebbles beneath her feet. "I'd like to get back before the sunlight runs out."

Sidra hated the darkness on a new world. Something in the shadows left her feeling unnerved. She had outgrown the imaginary monsters from her youth, but new ones could be born out in the distant corners of the universe.

The landscape was wide open and mainly empty on the return trip, except for the rock formations rising from the ground like giant fingers. There was a beauty to rocks, as if they held onto the colors of the sun. Further along, the rock formations grew larger with longer stretches of emptiness between. The rocks formed mountainous structures shaped like monuments to some forgotten gods. Sidra knew it couldn't be true, though. All reports from First Wave had described the native life as barely intelligent, only smart enough to kill, eat and reproduce. They were tiny little creatures appropriately named Swarmers since they would *swarm* the patrols and attempt to surround hardened facilities. Sidra read terrifying accounts of the beasts trying to claw their way in like a mindless, coordinated organism. The Lift-speeder raced past a grouping of massive boulders piled at the base of a steep rocky hill. Without warning, Mikken spun the craft around, quickly reducing speed.

"Mikken!" Sidra fussed.

"I'm sorry, my love," he apologized. "I've just seen something worth investigating."

This was code for a pretty plant. She didn't mind. She enjoyed watching him pursue his passions. Besides, they still had plenty of sunlight left to return to headquarters. Mikken lowered the speeder gently to the ground, and they both jumped out. They made their way between two of the larger boulders to a patch of green stalks with a blazing red flower adorning each one.

"Oh, those are actually quite pretty," Sidra noted. "What shall we call them, my love?"

"Sidra's Fire," Mikken smiled.

She had to admit; she was quite fond of the title.

"Hmm, what's that?" Mikken asked.

Further back behind the nearest boulder, set into the base of the rock hill, was the shadowy opening of a cave. Sidra could see from Mikken's face he wanted to go inside, a prospect she was apt to avoid.

"Mikken, maybe we shouldn't," she cautioned.

"The Swarmers are gone, my love," he said jovially. First Wave took care of them."

"Don't you think they could have missed a few?" she asked.

"They haven't yet," he reminded her. He was grinding his boot into the sand, trying to hide his impatience.

She found herself without another counter-argument that didn't come across as childish fear, so she relented and followed him forward.

The mouth of the cave was low, forming a frowning scar in the rock that made them crouch to avoid hitting their heads. Mikken and Sidra turned on lights built into their helmets, casting bright beams into the darkness. The sandy ground was disturbed by dozens of tracks, some featuring boot prints proportionate to their own, while others were much smaller. There were deep grooves akin to wheel marks Sidra thought might belong to a cart. She dropped to one knee, examining a set of the smaller prints while Mikken ventured further into the cave. Sidra was no expert when it came to studying animals, but she had a basic understanding of bipeds versus quadrupeds. The dominant race had been classified as quadrupedal, unintelligent, and highly aggressive. The more Sidra studied the tracks, they all seemed to belong to animals that walked on two feet.

"Sidra!" Mikken's voice called into her helmet speaker. "Sidra!" he called again, the fear coming through in his voice.

"I'm coming!" she yelled, rising and sprinting ahead, not pausing to consider what danger might be waiting.

The path curved to the left, then cut back sharply to the right. She was on him instantly, colliding into his back, knocking them both to the sandy floor.

"What is it?" she demanded, helping to roll him onto his back. She pawed at his visor, wiping away sand for a better look. "Are you hurt? Mikken!"

Mikken grabbed her wrists and held her steady. "Sidra, I'm fine!"

"Well then, what's the matter with you!" she scolded, slapping at his chest.

Mikken looked over his shoulder, shining his light into the open cave beyond. Sidra followed his gaze with hers, settling onto the largest piles of bones she had ever seen. Not that she had seen many piles of bones in her life, but the sheer number before her was staggering. There were thousands, perhaps tens of thousands, of skeletal pieces.

"Mikken, what is this?" Sidra asked, horrified.

Mikken crawled on hands and knees several feet forward and lifted a tiny skull in his hands, carefully rotating it with his fingers.

"Gods above and below, Sidra, they look like we do, only… smaller," he said.

Sidra moved in close behind him to get a better look. The skull was a fourth of the size of hers, which at first made her think it might be a child's skull. Only when she saw even smaller sets of bones did she realize she and Mikken were giants by comparison. The skull had more teeth, and the eye sockets were proportionately larger. The skull cavities didn't seem to have the chambers associated with processing chemicals for respiration.

"Look at the hand there," Sidra said, pointing to an intact arm nearby. "They don't seem to have their secondary thumb."

"God's Sidra, you know what this means?" he asked, turning

towards her. She stared blankly, unsure which of the many responses he was looking for. "It means First Wave lied!"

The implications were disturbing. The pile of bodies was not made up of mindless animals; they were an intelligent species, one Sidra might actually share some distance genetic relation with. If that was true, then her leadership was lying to their people. They were stealing planets from species far outside the threshold for recolonization. They were committing xenocide, and she was an accomplice.

"Mikken, what do we do?" she asked.

"We've got to get back to Sulamor and get a message to the World Speaker," Mikken said.

"Sulamor? You want to return all the way to our home world?" she asked.

"We can't risk sending a message from this solar system," he replied. "The transmission will be intercepted, jammed, and then First Wave will come for us. World Speaker has the equipment and the protection to broadcast to all the worlds simultaneously. The Pathfinders won't be able to ignore the accusation. They will be forced to answer for what they've done. We've been expanding across the galaxy for centuries. Image how many times this might have happened."

Sidra thought about Stack One, spewing carbon monoxide and nitrogen dioxide into the atmosphere, making the air breathable to her people. The oxygen levels were still too high to withstand, exacerbated by the plants that continued to convert carbon dioxide back into more oxygen. That's where Mikken came in, identifying the plant species that would need to be neutralized or replaced, and finding ways to incorporate their own plant species into a foreign environment. Seeing how she and her partner fit into the grand scheme made her feel dirty and blind, even willfully ignorant, for so many years.

"Mikken, what you're suggesting..." Sidra trailed off. The ruling body that led her people across the universe, the Pathfinders, did not look kindly at those who chose to stray.

Mikken offered her the tiny skull, but she did not move to

take it. "This could be our little one," he said solemnly. "They could be us," he waved over the pile of countless dead.

The rush of guilt started to overpower Sidra's fear for their lives. "We'd have to be careful," she warned. "We can't change our habits. We must conduct ourselves just as we always have. We can tell the Pathfinders we are returning home to share the news of our new traveler." Sidra rested a hand on her stomach.

Mikken smiled and nodded. "Of course, my love," he agreed. "Your safety is my primary concern."

Mikken returned the skull gently to the ground and stood, helping Sidra to her feet. "We should get back," he said.

As they made their way back to the cave entrance, Sidra paused, holding Mikken's hand at arm's length. "Do you think there are more piles...like this...other sites where they stacked the dead?"

Mikken turned to face her, looking grim. "Yes, my love. We should assume there's many."

After a few somber moments, they left the cave in a single file and got into the Lift-speeder without saying a word. Mikken flew, racing along a wide basin with gentle slopes on each side.

"Mikken..." Sidra began, feeling a tightness building in her chest.

Mikken placed a hand against her shoulder, then tapped the tiny comm antenna on the back of his helmet. Sidra understood. They would soon be, if not already, back in the listening range of command. They couldn't risk openly discussing the cave any longer. They had almost made their way out of the small valley when Mikken made a strange grunt as the Lift-speeder swerved from left to right.

"Mikken!" Sidra shouted, startled by his erratic driving.

She turned to look at him. There was a small, slender shaft sticking out below his collarbone. He had one hand gripping the material of his suit around the long stick to keep his air supply from leaking out.

"Mikken, what is that?" she asked, slightly dumbstruck.

The speeder began to veer to the right as beads of blood

dribbled out between his clenched fingers.

"God's Mikken, pull over!" she yelled.

There was a glint of light ahead, and another shaft struck Mikken with a thud in the center of his chest. Sidra screamed as the speeder jerked off course. The front right corner grazed an outcropping of rock, and there was an explosion of sound and a mighty shove of recoil. The speeder was thrown into a tight spin through the air, blurring Sidra's vision into streaks of brown and red. Sidra reached for Mikken as the craft's other front lift blade shut off, sending the front of the speeder into the ground. Sidra felt a surge of pain in her wrist and head, and everything turned black.

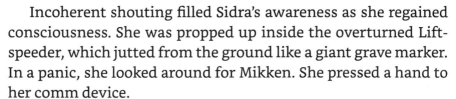

Incoherent shouting filled Sidra's awareness as she regained consciousness. She was propped up inside the overturned Lift-speeder, which jutted from the ground like a giant grave marker. In a panic, she looked around for Mikken. She pressed a hand to her comm device.

"Mikken," she breathed.

An angry growl filled her ears, then the straining sound of exertion. A small shape soared through the air overhead, little arms and legs flailing as it came crashing down on a flat stone partially buried in the sand. There was a loud smack as its head broke open, painting the tan stone red. Sidra jumped as another object crashed into the back side of the speeder. She scrambled to her feet, cradling her broken wrist against her body, trying not to topple over as her vision swam from her head injury. Sidra rounded the front of the overturned speeder to see a primal battle playing out.

Mikken had one of the swarmers, the living version of the bones they had found, held by one of its legs as he swung it like a club. He swatted another long-haired swarmer clear off the ground. It flipped backward, landing in a motionless heap in the sand. The "Swarmers", as First Wave had named them, were definitely bipedal. The similarities between their species and her own were alarming. The long-haired figure had seemed female, having a smaller frame and pronounced breasts. She had two arms and two legs, just like Sidra. There were three others with shorter hair and larger muscles, two holding pointed sticks, while one had a crudely made bow. The one with the primitive bow pointed an arrow in Sidra's direction. Mikken yelled and jumped between the arrow's flight path as it was released towards Sidra, throwing his arms out in front of him. The shaft struck through the top of his right hand.

"Mikken!" Sidra screamed, frozen with shock and terror.

Mikken stood, his suit pockmarked with holes and a half dozen tiny arrows stuck into his arms and chest. He was gasping for air, but when he saw Sidra, it was like a fire had been lit inside him. He spun and dashed across the sand, taking an arrow in the thigh but giving it no attention. He was on the figure with the bow, using the arrow protruding from his hand to punch its body, quickly turning its faded blue and white shirt into red. One of the spear holders ran in fear while the other charged at Mikken from behind, preparing to stick him in the lower back. Sidra moved as if she had teleported instead of run; her hands were clasped around a thin, brittle neck, squeezing her fingers together like a prayer for death.

"Sidra," a weak voice spoke through the comms. "Let him go."

Sidra looked beyond the lifeless Swarmer between her hands. Mikken was slumped over on his knees several paces ahead.

"My love!" she screamed, dropping the body and rushing to his side.

His suit was ruined, and several arrows had punctured his lungs. Death would be arriving shortly. Sidra began to take off her suit. "I'll walk with you to the final gate, my love."

"No," he labored, placing a hand on her belly. "Finish the path…for her."

Mikken died cradled in Sidra's arms. She let out a scream of anguish, pulling him close against her chest.

A static crackled into her helmet speaker. "Sidra! This is

Command. We've identified your comms. What's happening?"

"We were attacked," Sidra said, looking at Mikken. "It was the Swarmers."

"Attacked?" The voice asked. "The Swarmers were completely wiped out in your sector long before the construction of Stack One!"

"They've returned," she said weakly.

"Are you hurt?" command asked. "Where's Mikken?"

"He's gone down the final path...where I can't follow," she cried.

"I'm alerting First Wave," the voice said. "We'll destroy every trace of those beasts!"

There was movement at the corner of Sidra's vision. A part of her, an overwhelming majority, wished the second Swarmer with a spear had returned to finish her off. Mikken had wanted her to live, but he hadn't had time to consider the loneliness she would have to endure. Sidra turned to scan a low outcropping of rock nearby. She was stunned to see a small scruff of hair accompanying a set of tiny eyes. Sidra remained motionless, watching in wonder as the little figure crept out from behind its cover and moved toward the dead bodies on the ground.

The Swarmers Mikken and Sidra had fought were small, but the one she saw now was a fraction of their size.

"A child," Sidra whispered.

The figure crept across the ground, moving to the closest body of a slain warrior in the sand. The child, a dark-haired male, shook the dead warrior by the arm, speaking a language she didn't understand.

"Sidra, do you hear me?" Command asked over comms. "We're sending First Wave."

"No!" she shouted. "Do not send First Wave," she ordered. "Send retrievers for the dead, but not First Wave. There is no more blood to spill."

She was helping to build a new future for her own babies while stealing hope from the ones already living on the planet. Sidra looked toward Stack One in the distance, spewing several chemicals unbreathable to the native species. The new Swarmers had two, maybe three years before their air became unbreathable. She felt a sudden flood of shame and disgust. Swarmers had been deemed primitive creatures, violent and debased, incapable of higher thinking.

The child stood upright at the sound of Sidra's voice, watching her with a cautious and unwavering stare. Sidra gently laid Mikkens head onto the sand and bolted towards the child, reaching him in several strides. The child fell back into the sand, baring his teething and shouting words she couldn't understand. His knees and elbows shook. He was terrified of her. From his perspective, *she* was the monster. Sidra crouched low, digging her knees into the sand as she tried to look less imposing. She had never interacted with an intelligent alien species before.

She patted her chest. "Sidra," she said. "Sidra." She repeated the gesture. Sidra looked back to where Mikken's body lay in the sand. "Mikken," she said through tears. She pointed at his body. "Mikken."

The child looked at her and patted his chest. "James." He looked at the dead warrior, producing tears of his own. He laid a hand gently on the dead Swarmer's head. "Dad," the boy said. "Tom."

Sidra pointed to the dead figure. "Dad Tom," She repeated.

James, assuming that was his name, shook his head. "Tom."

Sidra wasn't sure of the distinction, but she pointed at him, saying "James", then the warrior, saying "Tom".

James nodded in confirmation. Sidra pointed to the clear sky in the direction of her home world. "Sulamor," she said, then pointed at the ground, shrugging her shoulders. She repeated the word and the gesture, then waited.

James dug his fingers into the sand. "Earth," he said, gripping two large handfuls. "Earth."

"Earth," Sidra said, rising to her feet.

She turned away from the child and looked out on the horizon, watching Stack One spewing its billowing white and grey clouds into the air. Her eyes scanned and strained, barely making out Stack Two as a blurry apparition in the distance. She looked back at James to find him clinging to the dead warrior, most likely his father. She returned to the side of her love, Mikken, and lay beside him in the sand. She prayed to the gods above and below to set things right. It was too late for so many things, but never to forge a new path. All it took was the first step in a different direction. In her heart, Sidra knew which way she was headed.

V. HISTORICAL FICTION

"I have always regarded historical fiction and fantasy as sisters under the skin, two genres separated at birth." - George R. R. Martin

THE SHADOW MAID

F lakes of ash drifted down from a cloudy sky, peppering the rooftops and the roads, mixing into cold puddles in the mud. On some days, the ash was everywhere, oppressive with its ceaseless rain upon our heads to remind us of fate's cruel hand and the absence of God. We, of course, had parasols to keep our clothes from being stained from the relentless soot, although the prisoners barely had scraps of fabric to serve as uniforms or strips of beaten leather to call a shoe. The smokestack of the Dachau crematorium was an obscene obelisk in the sky, spewing out the charred remains of great thinkers, painters, doctors, lovers, grandparents, and even children; all that life and hope was ripped away. The architect of these horrors, Heinrich Himmler, possibly the most powerful man next to Hitler, stood out on the balcony of his villa, set a half mile from the camp's walls. He looked out proudly at his accomplishments, the sheer scale of the atrocities he had helped to engineer. He turned to me and smiled. It was warm and genuine and made the hairs stand up on the back of my neck. He extended an empty teacup in my direction, watching me expectantly. I don't know how I kept my hands from shaking, but I managed a steady pour that left his cup full and steaming.

"Thank you, Heidi," he said, turning away to look back on that man-made hell.

I gave a little dip of gratitude, even though his back was already turned to me. You never knew who was looking, and appearances must always be maintained. A distant echo of gunfire from the camp made me flinch. It must have been time for executions. Himmler stood unmoved as I steadied myself back into my attentive, servile posture. I stared at the back of a killer, praying his heart would stop, but it kept beating. I often prayed for the strength and the courage to grab his service pistol from his hip and put a round into the back of his skull, but my courage failed then, as it often did. What could I do? I was nobody; I was just a simple housemaid.

In the summer of 1943, there were four of us at the start: Jennifer Warnecke, Eva Köpp, Hannah Dieterich, and me. We had all been carefully vetted to ensure we were "purebred" German women of reputable backgrounds. We were tasked with providing cleaning services to high-ranking officers so they could continue to perform their duties, unencumbered by the time-consuming menial tasks of domestic labor. It was fairly easy to become detached at first, staying busy with the house and the grounds, listening to stories about the detestable nature of the prisoners and how good men like Himmler were doing their part for the safety of our great nation. It was near Christmas time, and Hannah was setting an advent wreath on the kitchen table when the first group of prisoners was ushered into the house.

"What are you doing?" Himmler's voice boomed at a pair of SS Guards flanking a disheveled group of six gaunt prisoners. "Around back, damn you! Just look at these floors!"

Indeed, the floor around the guards' boots and the prisoners' bare feet was smeared in streaks of dark mud. I could see the tension in the prisoners' bodies, although they dared not to look up to meet the anger of Himmler's gaze. The guards quickly ushered the men back out the front door and around the back of the villa as Himmler stepped forward and over the dirt, spinning around to show an apologetic smile.

"Ladies, ignore this intrusion," he said, more like an order than any sort of apology. "We are putting a garden in the back.

Although those men know little of art and beauty, they will help us create it. Do not be alarmed by their presence. They should know better than to walk through the house."

"It's quite alright," Eva said, flashing an embellished smile. "Besides, you and the guards will keep us safe!" she exclaimed.

I felt the compulsion to slap her but pulled at the threading on my sleeve instead. Himmler looked Eva up and down like a showhorse, then gave a smirking look of approval that made her blush. Hannah rolled her eyes and went to fetch a mop and bucket. I stayed behind to help her clean.

Later that evening, I stood alone in the kitchen looking out on the back of the property, watching those poor men as they toiled with shovels and pickaxes in the biting cold. They were given neither work boots nor gloves, and the guards buzzed around them like angry hornets, offering insults and harsh critiques of their work as the prisoners shrank back at threats of violence. I washed vegetables absentmindedly in the sink, unable to tear my eyes away from the pitiful work detail. The guards were bundled up in thick winter coats, shouting at the men to hurry up before they missed that night's meal when one of the pickaxes sank into the frosted ground and gave a loud snap as the metal head broke from the shaft.

The man with the tool looked up, holding the broken wood handle, and his face reminded me of a guilty child who had just been caught stealing from his father's wallet. He turned to the other prisoners, but they wouldn't meet his eye. He faced the nearest guard and was struck across the temple, dropping him to the floor. I gasped at the brutal overreaction. The tools were old and worn, the ground frozen into hard chunks of icy mud, yet the guards set upon him as if he had snapped the tool deliberately and with spite. It was the first true beating I had ever witnessed, but it certainly wouldn't be the last. As the two guards finally finished and were dragging the man's limp body away, I had the most curious compulsion come over me. I cracked open the kitchen window and tossed out several carrots I had been preparing to cut. I was frozen with the shock of my actions, and for a time, so were the prisoners standing unsupervised in the backyard. One man, who looked twenty years old, yet somehow also in his sixties, shuffled forward and scooped up the carrots. He stuffed one into a hidden pocket on his shirt and passed off the other to a man who snapped the carrot in half and hid the pieces under each armpit. Then, without further word and a discreet nod in my direction, they trudged back around the house and were gone.

My small acts of defiance continued from there, often manifesting in secretive donations of food and soft smiles offered to counter the sneers and tongue lashings the workers received daily. Several weeks after the garden project began, the maid staff was tasked with additional laundry duty for the guards and officers at the camp. Large industrial washers and dryers were installed on the ground floor, along with ramps that entered a garage area and exited at a loading dock at the back of the property. A large white bread truck came to take away the cleaned linens on Thursdays or Fridays. While none of us looked forward to taking on more duties, I volunteered so that I might be spared the heartbreaking view of the men outside. Eva and Jennifer seemed quite pleased to pass on the work, although Hannah offered to help whenever I needed it. I soon learned that looking away changed nothing for their suffering, and I had already become swept up in their plans for freedom.

Finding a child concealed inside a laundry bin was the last thing I expected on the second week into the new year, but there he was, staring up with fearful watery eyes. His skin was papery thin, wrapped around protruding cheekbones. His eyes had a rich blue hue that hadn't faded, despite his appearance. He offered a small scrap of paper that said, 'Trust the driver. Please help'.

The driver's name was Otto, a burly man who kept a small swastika sign on his back left window. He was the last man I would have accused of helping Dachau prisoners escape, which I suppose was the point. For months we smuggled out children, sometimes two or three at once. I was terrified every time a laundry bin was wheeled into the house, but each success emboldened me further and filled me with a sense of purpose I had

never known.

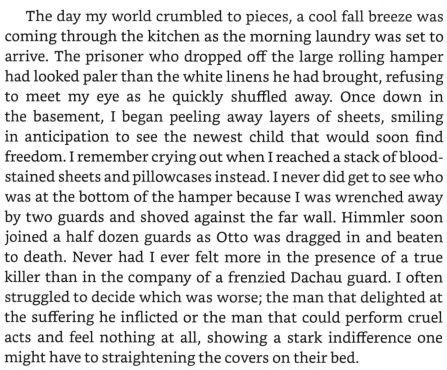

The day my world crumbled to pieces, a cool fall breeze was coming through the kitchen as the morning laundry was set to arrive. The prisoner who dropped off the large rolling hamper had looked paler than the white linens he had brought, refusing to meet my eye as he quickly shuffled away. Once down in the basement, I began peeling away layers of sheets, smiling in anticipation to see the newest child that would soon find freedom. I remember crying out when I reached a stack of blood-stained sheets and pillowcases instead. I never did get to see who was at the bottom of the hamper because I was wrenched away by two guards and shoved against the far wall. Himmler soon joined a half dozen guards as Otto was dragged in and beaten to death. Never had I ever felt more in the presence of a true killer than in the company of a frenzied Dachau guard. I often struggled to decide which was worse; the man that delighted at the suffering he inflicted or the man that could perform cruel acts and feel nothing at all, showing a stark indifference one might have to straightening the covers on their bed.

When the guards had finished, and Otto lay unmoving in a crimson pool, Himmler turned to me and said casually, "Since you love them so much, tomorrow you will join them in the gas chamber." That was the last time I ever saw him. Afterward, I was locked in my quarters by the guards and was told they would retrieve me in the morning. That night Hannah came to me, slipping a sheet of paper and pencil under the door, crying as she told me she would deliver the letter to my family when she could. Maybe my parents would have understood why I helped those children, but maybe not. Instead, I wrote to whoever might listen on the side of the Allies. I pray to God that if he truly exists, my letter will find its way to the Supreme Commander of the Allied Forces via sympathizers within the Swedish Red Cross. Although I now face the strong certainty of death, let it be known that I did so with my chin raised high and fierce defiance burning in my heart. There are persisting rumors that Himmler has fallen out of favor with Hitler, but I do not know the exact circumstances. It is said, even now, that he has been making plans to depart from Dachau and flee like the coward he is. Throughout my year and a half of service to Heinrich Himmler, I overheard him say on several occasions that he had contacts in the town of Bremervorde that could help smuggle him out of Germany to safety.

While I have no doubts the world would be a better place without Himmler, a small part of me wants him to flee, if only to give him the same false sense of hope he helped to force upon so many. If fate may have it that he does flee from justice, only to be caught as a rat in hiding, do share with him that I, Heidi Meinhardt, betrayed his whereabouts. Not a spy of great skill or soldier of legendary heroics, but me, a simple maid working in the shadows.

BEAUTIFUL
LITTLE FOOL

"Hello, suckers! Come on in and leave your wallet on the bar!" Texas shouted at a group of finely dressed gentlemen as they entered the 300 Club. *Her* club.

The men laughed and hooted. One even reached into his inner jacket pocket and produced a fat billfold stuffed to the brink with hundreds. He waved it in the air like he might start passing out Benjamins to the crowd. There was a pregnant, hopeful silence that swelled and popped as he laughed and slipped the billfold back inside his coat. If it had been a year prior, it would have been the most money Betty had ever seen at once. Working for the famed Texas Guinan, well, it was just another Friday night.

Betty zipped through the crowd, balancing a tray holding a dozen shots of gin. The rolling sounds of the night's jazz ensemble filled the air with a frantic energy that felt electric. Betty bounced and hopped to the rhythm, half dancing the liquor across the room as the tray perched precariously on her fingertips. She ducked around several of the other girls who were dancing the shimmy to the joyful shouting of the crowd. They looked like triplets in their short sequin dresses, bright red lipstick, and shingle haircuts. Betty preferred the bob herself, but the short skirts did make it a hell of a lot easier to move about. She'd be dancing later that night while Texas sat at the bar, singing and casting playful insults to some of the most powerful men in the city.

This is living, Betty thought. She was nineteen and ready to take on the world. She could vote, drink, smoke, and stay out all night. Her parents would be horrified, but they were almost seven hundred miles away, living a simple life back home in North Carolina. Here, beneath the bright lights of New York City, the sky was the limit, and she was ready to see how far she could go.

A loud smack and the sting of a handprint on her backside yanked her head from the clouds. She turned to see some zozzled fool, grinning like an idiot, hand still raised in an innocent wave. His wedding ring stood out, making the indignity worse.

"Hey there, honey," he slurred. "It's my birthday. How 'bout a dance for me and the boys!"

Two other men at the table cheered.

"Go chase yourself!" she shot back. "I'm sure your wife is waiting up."

Betty didn't mind when the men got rowdy, but she hated when they got handsy. Texas told the girls to check the ones that got out of line but not to run them off. When the boys were drunk and happy, the liquor and the tips would flow.

The red-faced man blushed as his friends laughed and slapped his back. Betty let that be the end of it and turned away to drop off the shots at the far end of the dining room. She took the long way back to the bar and grabbed a glass of water and a small stack of bar napkins to dab at the sweat on her forehead.

Blazes, it's hot tonight, she thought. She watched Red Face, standing in his chair as his friends howled out the opening lines to 'happy birthday'. The whole place, feeling tipsy and gay, joined in, and soon even Texas was singing along. Betty took another sip of water and frowned.

"What's up, Betty?" her friend Millie asked as she reached behind the bar for two fresh glasses. "Why the long face?"

"That guy the club is singing to," Betty said as the crowd mumbled through 'Dear Harry'. "He's just being a creep."

The band squawked out the last notes of the birthday song as the crowd and Harry gave a cheerful round of applause.

"Do you want me to grab the doorman?" Millie asked. "I think Bobby's here tonight. He'll sort him out."

Betty sighed. "No, I'm fine, thanks. They just get excited sometimes. Anyways, I need the tips. Rent won't pay itself."

Another half dozen suits came in through the front door. They were the gangster type, sporting tailored Brooks Brothers suits and matching hats. Texas rushed to meet them, embracing a hard-looking fellow in the lead, then guided them to the VIP section by the right side of the main stage.

"Who's that?" Betty asked, watching the crowd part to let them pass.

"Who's that?" Millie repeated. "That's Owney Madden. He runs the booze for Texas; he helped set her up in the 300. Make sure you don't forget that one!" Millie rushed off, leaving Betty to stare and wonder.

Betty buzzed in and out past Red Face's, now known as Harry's, table as quickly as she could. Harry was one of those successful Wall Street types. He had money to spend and didn't miss a chance to show it off. As annoying as he could be, types like him were good for business. The drunker they got, the more they liked to spend. If Betty played her cards right, she might have the entire month's rent tucked in her purse by the night's end. She noticed Ruth weaving her way to the bar, looking flustered as she scanned a notepad like it might be full of trigonometry problems instead of drink orders.

"Ruthie, are you alright?" Betty asked, raising her voice to compete with the music.

"Betty, can I get a hand in VIP?" Ruth asked, teetering around the point of exasperation. "I just got double seated, and I can barely keep up as it is. We can split the tips; I'm drowning here!"

Betty didn't have the heart to say no and didn't want to turn down extra tips to boot.

"Um, sure thing," Betty said, feeling a sudden rush of nerves.

Betty copied the order, grabbed two pitchers of beer in one hand and a stack of glasses in the other, and made her way to the roped-off VIP table. One of the six men jumped up and unclipped the rope to let her in. He was young, handsome, and couldn't be much older than she was. He had a pointed toothpick set in the corner of his mouth that he shifted from left to right. He was clean-shaven, his skin smooth and unblemished, except for a small, pink scar etched into the right side of his chin. All the details registered in a heartbeat, but his eyes made her linger. They looked almost silver, large, and fixed upon her as she moved to where Owney Madden sat.

"What's the matter, Ruth, didn't wanna see me no more?" Owney asked, feigning a look of hurt.

"Oh, nothing like that, Mr. Madden. She just got busy, is all," Betty quickly replied.

"I'm just joshing, doll. Ruth's a good kid." He turned to one of his stooges. The man had a square jaw and a flat nose. "I still say it's your ugly mug that ran her off."

The other men laughed and pointed as Betty poured the first beer for Owney.

"Ah, you don't have to do that, love," Owney said. "The boys will get it. Danny boy, help the lady!"

Danny, the young man that had held the rope, stepped up and took the pitcher, his hands briefly brushing Betty's. She felt a flush of heat, and not from the thrush of patrons drinking and dancing to the sounds of an upbeat jazz number.

"What's your name?" Danny asked, shifting his toothpick from the right to the left.

"Betty," she replied, then smiled and hurried away to check on her other tables.

Betty chanced a look back, and Danny was still standing, a hint of a smile as he watched her with those eyes like rings of moonlight.

The night went on, and the food and drink service paused as the girls lined up to kick off an energetic showing of the Charleston as Texas sat on top of the bar, clapping approvingly. Harry and his Wall Street pals were still loitering around, trying to lure girls to sit at their table with the promise of free drinks. The dance ended, and Betty felt the room sway. It was hot, and she hadn't had any water to drink over the last hour. She made for an empty table to sit but was cut off by Harry, drunker than ever.

"It's my birthday!" he reminded her, clumsily pawing at her hands. "Dance with me!" he smiled, eyes barely focused.

"Oh, I couldn't," Betty protested, moving back to the chair.

Harry clutched her hands in his and insistently pulled her back towards the dance floor.

"You're zozzled, mister, now turn me loose!" she protested, her voice drowned out by the band.

Harry kept pulling, and she kept leaning the other way, trying not to make a scene. Harry's grip slipped, and Betty tumbled to the floor, skinning her knees on the polished wood. Harry was laughing like a jackass but didn't bother to help her. The air was thick as hot soup, and it felt like the whole room was laughing as the other patrons danced circles around her, too drunk and caught up in the revelry to pay her any mind. Texas didn't look kindly on the girls crying, but right then, Betty felt like she could dash from the club and never come back.

Just then, a dark blur flashed past the edge of her vision. Betty heard a commotion and the sound of glass breaking. The music had stopped before she finished turning to look. Danny had moved across the entire dance floor and had Harry's face pinned down on top of his table, one hand tangled up in his hair. Danny's other hand pinched his toothpick between thumb and forefinger, and the point was an inch from going into Harry's left eye. Every soul in the 300 Club seemed to be holding their breath. Two large bouncers made a move for Danny but were waved off by Texas as she hopped from the bar and slowly made her way to the edge of the dance floor. Betty saw Owney standing on the opposite end of the crowd; the rest of his crew were silent observers with oversized coats draped over their right hands. Danny spoke in a low voice into Harry's ear, and Harry tried his best to nod under the weight of Danny's hand pressing on his face. Harry's two Wall Street buddies stood by, helpless to intervene, well aware of the line of gangsters twenty feet away.

Harry awkwardly reached into his pocket and tossed several ten-dollar bills onto the table, then yelped as Danny pressed his head harder into the wooden table. Harry threw a money clip of larger bills onto the table and awkwardly held up two hands.

"That's all!" Harry insisted. "I swear!"

Danny whispered several more words into Harry's ear, then let the man up. Harry stood and swayed, one side of his face red, the other wet from spilled liquor on the table.

"I'm real sorry, Ms. Betty. I was a damned fool!" Harry whined. "Please accept my tip for your troubles. I'd better see myself home."

Harry looked to Danny, who nodded his approval, also giving him permission to leave. Harry's two pals joined him, and they slunk out the front entrance like scolded children. The room breathed a collective sigh of relief as Texas made herself the center of attention on the dance floor.

"Well, wasn't that exciting!" she cried out, eliciting a few nervous laughs. "Looks like someone was just a bit too smoked tonight." There were more laughs. "How about a free round on your old pal Texas, and we get this party back on track!" she bellowed.

The jazz band wasted no time, launching into a rendition of the Shanghai Shuffle by Fletcher Henderson as the rest of the girls rushed to the bar for glasses and pitchers. Betty felt dizzy with the commotion, unsure if she should stand up or sit on the floor for another spell. Danny stood over her and offered a hand. He hoisted her up with muscular arms, holding her close as she found her bearings once more.

"Are you alright?" Danny asked, in a cool, even New York accent.

"I'm fine, thank you," she said, still shaken from the thought of Danny plucking out Harry's eye like an olive. "I...I should get back to work." She broke away and hurriedly added. "Thank you."

Danny's eyes lingered on her for several moments before he replaced his toothpick between his lips and strode back towards

Owney and his crew. The music played on, and the drinks continued to flow until the early hours of the morning.

Betty woke up to the smell of bacon, eggs, and freshly brewed coffee. She rolled over to Danny's side of the bed. Empty again. Betty didn't know how a person could stay out as late as he did, get a few hours of sleep, then be back up on their feet and ready to face the next day before the sun came up. But that was Danny. They had been seeing each other for over a month, and things were going better than she could have ever hoped for. Millie had protested, saying that Danny's crew was just a bunch of thugs, but they didn't dress like thugs. Danny certainly didn't act like one, not around her, at least. He was kind and gentle but also strong and fearless. When they were out in public together, it made her feel untouchable. Nobody cat-called her or came up to pester her for a date. Even the men at the club treated her with nothing but respect. Eventually, Harry had returned to the 300 Club, walking through the door like he had received a personal invite from Texas herself. She greeted him with a jovial insult, sat him and his two cronies at a nice table, and that was that. All had been forgiven; water under the bridge. The drinks were poured, and Harry was all smiles. When he finally made eye contact with Betty, he smiled, gave a polite tip of his hat, and waited patiently for his next round. Danny had been in the club that night, but Harry had transformed into the perfect gentleman even when he wasn't.

Betty wobbled into the kitchen wearing one of Danny's loose shirts; her head was still foggy from the night before. Duke Ellington, *the* Duke Ellington, had been playing, and the crowd had partied and danced like they were out on parole. Danny stood over the stove top, spatula in his left hand, cigarette in his right. He was wearing a pair of black and red checkered flannel pants but no shirt. He was tall and lean, the muscles in his back moving with the rhythm coming from the radio above the stove.

He took a drag from the cigarette and noticed her enter the room as he exhaled.

"Morning, beautiful," he said, eyeing her over. "Too much giggle water last night?"

Betty grumbled and shuffled forward, pressing herself against his back and wrapping her arms around his stomach. Danny offered her the cigarette, and she took a long drag. The smoke tasted bitter, but it settled her stomach and deflated some of the pressure in her head.

"I'm never drinking again," she groaned.

"You said that last weekend," he teased.

"Yeah, well, this time, I mean it."

Danny turned and kissed her lightly on the forehead.

"Have a seat," he said, "I'll make you a plate."

Betty knew when Danny cooked this early, it usually meant he had to run errands and drive Owney around town in his Rolls Royce. It made her worry, but he assured her he was safe and Owney only bought the car to impress women.

"You know, one of these days, you're going to have to play for me," Betty said, moving her eggs around on the plate.

"Play what?" he asked, looking confused.

"The violin, silly. I saw the case in the closet when I was grabbing a shirt," she said.

His puzzlement lingered for another moment, and then a silly grin spread across his face. A low chuckle grew into a hearty laugh.

"Oh right, yeah, I play sometimes. I only know the one song, though," he mused.

Betty smiled back but soon soured when she realized she was the butt of the joke.

"Don't tease me!" she scolded.

Danny laughed, putting his hands up in surrender. "I'm sorry, Betty, I'm just having a laugh. Fetch me the case, babe."

Betty retrieved the case, noting the weight as she entered the kitchen. The fog of her hangover was lifting, and by the time Danny flipped the latches open, she guessed what was in the case as a polished Tommy Gun stared back at her.

"Are you some kind of triggerman?" she asked, looking back at him.

Danny cleared his throat and took his time pulling smoke from the cigarette. "Nothing like that, just for protection," he said. "Owney gave one to all the guys."

"He's a regular Saint Nick, giving presents to his boys," she ribbed.

"What, you want a chopper for Christmas?" Danny teased back.

"Would you teach me?" Betty asked.

"To shoot?" he asked.

"Why not?" she asked indignantly.

Danny paused, thinking, then wrapped her up in a firm embrace. "Sure, why not." He kissed her forehead, then her right cheek, then softly across the lips. "But first, breakfast."

December in New York was frigid, but a light snowfall gave the night an air of magic. Texas had let Betty off early to celebrate her one-year anniversary with Danny. He looked at her lightweight jacket on the way out of the 300 Club, shook his head, and threw his heavy overcoat around her shoulders. He dropped his hat onto her head from an exaggerated height, making her giggle as she struck a tough pose.

"Come on, Capone, let's get you in the car," he said.

Danny led her to a familiar Rolls Royce parked in front of the club.

"Danny, is that...?" Betty began.

"Owney's, yeah. He's letting me take you for a spin...to celebrate."

Danny was fidgeting with the buttons on his shirt. He had a nervousness that wasn't in his character. The look in his eyes told her it might just be a surprise that would send her over the moon. They left West 54th Street and headed south toward

Coney Island, where they had their first date. Halfway there, Danny started looking in the rearview mirror, occasionally at first, then frequently as they drove by Gravesend Bay on their right.

"Danny, what is it?" Betty asked.

"I think somebody is following us," he replied, with a hint of paranoia in his voice.

Betty looked back and was met with a pair of headlights fifty yards back, although they seemed as normal as any she came across in the city.

"How do you know?" she asked.

"I know," he said. "Betty, there's a case in the back seat behind me. I want you to grab it."

Betty looked, and there was a violin case just like Danny's. She hoisted it into her lap and looked to Danny for further instructions. The car behind them started flashing their lights in rapid succession but kept their distance. Danny frowned and focused on the review mirror. He looked back at the road ahead and shouted in surprise. Thirty yards ahead, two men in overcoats stood in the middle of the road holding machine guns. Danny grabbed one of Betty's shoulders and shoved her down as the two men opened fire on their car.

Bullets peppered the hood and struck the windshield, punching out holes and leaving spiderwebs of cracked glass as Betty screamed. Danny cried out in pain and lurched forward into the steering wheel as they jerked to the left and then back to the right, sliding on a thin film of snow. The car spun around, skittering backward as the brakes locked up. They came to a stop, facing in the direction of the shooters as Danny's door opened, and he spilled out from the driver's seat onto the road.

"Danny!" she screamed as dark shadows crept into the light ahead.

Betty flung open the case, grabbed the Tommy Gun, and leaned over the driver's seat cushion, pointing the barrel out the open door. She squeezed the trigger, and the gun hurled lead into the night, the barrel spitting tiny fires as the recoil rattled her chest. The two men coming towards her made a funny dance, all jerky motions, then crumpled to the ground as they became gray shapes below the headlights of the Rolls Royce. Betty crawled forward out of the car to where Danny lay in the street. His shirt was soaked in blood, and he stared into the blackened sky as tiny snowflakes frosted him in white, melting and giving him a chill. With an effort, he turned his head towards the two stiffs on the road.

"That's...my girl," he strained.

"Oh, Danny," she cried, throwing his coat back over him like a blanket. "We've got to get to a hospital!"

"Betty, listen to me," he choked out. "There's going to be... more coming."

"What do I do?" she pleaded.

"You run," he said grimacing.

"I'm not leaving!" she shouted. "Not for anything."

Danny's eyes, those rings of moonlight, had closed, and he wasn't moving.

"Danny?" she asked, trembling.

A second pair of headlights appeared, the vehicle racing towards her like a bat out of hell.

"I ain't running," she hissed, grabbing the gun and standing.

She buried the stock into her shoulder like Danny had taught her and aimed down the sights.

"I ain't running!" she screamed into the night.

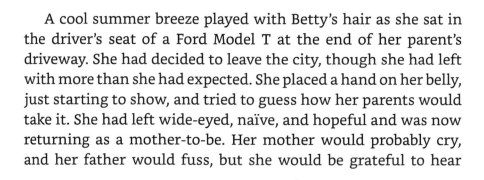

A cool summer breeze played with Betty's hair as she sat in the driver's seat of a Ford Model T at the end of her parent's driveway. She had decided to leave the city, though she had left with more than she had expected. She placed a hand on her belly, just starting to show, and tried to guess how her parents would take it. She had left wide-eyed, naïve, and hopeful and was now returning as a mother-to-be. Her mother would probably cry, and her father would fuss, but she would be grateful to hear their voices again. She had fought for her life and won it fair and square that cold winter night in the city. She had prayed that if she made it out alive, she would swear off the flapper lifestyle and live a life of simplicity, surrounded by the people she loved. She wasn't about to waste a second chance on worries now.

"Are you ready?" Betty asked, turning to her right.

Danny sat stiffly in the passenger seat, still healing from his wounds, frowning as he picked at his shirt. Danny sighed and produced a toothpick, placing it between his lips.

"What if they don't like me?" he asked. "What if they think I'm damned a fool."

"You *are* a damned fool," she smiled, putting a hand on his cheek. "But you're my fool." She held up the wedding ring for him to see. "And I'm yours."

"It's so quiet out here," he noted. "Are you sure you're ready to settle down?" he asked, eyeing his bride.

"I might have brought back a few bad habits," she mused, "assuming you can still cut a rug in your condition."

Danny grinned in silent acceptance of her challenge.

"Besides," she said, taking his hand and placing it over her stomach, "I have a feeling you're in for more excitement than you think."

ACKNOWLEDGEMENT

A heartfelt thank you to Chelsey Gillespie, Debbie Gillespie, Gary Westfal, and Janeen Westfal for all the beta reading, edits, and encouragement. I'd also like to thank Creag Monroe at Elegant Literature magazine for giving me my first professional publication. You made me feel like I had finally stepped across a threshold and could call myself an author. Thank you to all my friends and family who have supported my writing, and thank you to my girls. You motivate me to dream big and never give up.

ABOUT THE AUTHOR

Evan Gillespie

Evan lives in Florida with his wife Chelsey and four daughters, Rylee, Isabel, Sadie, and Ella. He has been writing and collecting stories for almost twenty years, dabbling in screenwriting, full-length novels, and short fiction. He has received multiple publications and recognitions for his short fiction, and has a forthcoming epic science fiction novel, The Endless Night. Additionally, he is crafting another ongoing science fiction series, Deep Space Crimes, has several side projects, and still writes short fiction for future World Builder Anthology volumes. How does he find time to accomplish all that writing, work full-time in the US Air Force, raise four wonderful daughters, and nerd out with books, hobbies, games, and movies? Caffeine, poor sleeping habits, and stubborn determination!

Made in the USA
Columbia, SC
02 September 2023

22407164R00129